I knew now why I was awake.

I could smell smoke.

Some smoke smells are delicious, but this wasn't an innocent smell.

I'm frightened of fire. Not everybody knows this about me, but people close to me, like Ben and Mrs. Twining, know that even to light a match costs me a pang. Now I could feel my throat tightening and my heart beating fast.

I opened my bedroom door and an evil frond of thick grey smoke curled up from the stairwell by my feet.

My house is small, the staircase narrow and curving, but I knew I had to go down it into that pit of smoke.

I could scream, but no one would hear. . . .

Ironwood

A NOVEL BY

Jennie Melville

A FAWCETT CREST BOOK

Fawcett Publications, Inc., Greenwich, Connecticut

IRONWOOD

THIS BOOK CONTAINS THE COMPLETE TEXT OF THE
ORIGINAL HARDCOVER EDITION.

A Fawcett Crest Book reprinted by arrangement with David
McKay Company, Inc.

Library of Congress Catalog Card Number: 72-81686

Printed in the United States of America

Ironwood

1

When the wind blew from the west across the narrow neck of land where I lived, it always seemed to me to bring with it a time of happiness. It was a gentle, sweet wind. But when it blew from the south, straight from the sea, bringing with it the gulls and the noise of heavy rollers, it seemed to herald a time of trouble. For a few weeks, before I became the person I am now, it must have blown from both quarters at once. Certainly it was a time in my life when I knew both terror and great joy. You could say for those weeks I was two people; one screaming, and the other hopelessly in love.

I have noticed that a period of change in one's life is often announced by the appearance of a new person. The time when my life began to break up into two schizophrenic parts began with the appearance of that subtle and sophisticated woman Lynn Alloway. She represented nothing major in my life, did nothing for me, did not, I guess, even like me, and yet hers was the hand that fate appointed to raise the curtain. For this reason I can never forget her.

But she fascinated me in herself. I saw her, it's impossible not to say it, as somebody out of a Victorian cause célèbre, a woman of whose motives we are never quite sure, who remains, always, a little bit of an enigma.

In this little corner of the woods violence of any sort, let alone violent crime, is virtually unknown, but death is the exception. Death can strike anywhere, can't it? No one is immune. You don't even have to be violent to be a killer, just desperate or unlucky, or possibly both. But perhaps the victim has to have a bag of violence inside him to call out murder. There's a whole field of study here.

In this beautiful place where I have lived and grown up among friends there are two strands, one of simplicity, the other of sophistication. We live in the country, but there is nothing rustic about our society, rather, it is mannered, elegant and rich. We own cows and can talk about heifers but we are no more farmers than was Marie Antoinette at Le Petit Trianon, and our dairies are decorated by David Hicks with a bit of sculpture by Paolozzi in the courtyard. My garden runs down to the meadow with Jersey cows in it, but between me and the beasts is a ditch. I think this is what my life has been like: between me and the world there has always been a hidden barrier. Did I put the barrier there myself? Or was it built for me by those remote ancestors of mine, like the gentle Scots knight who fell at Flodden and the little Tartar princess who rode with her father's hordes in Russia and married a Romanov?

We are about a dozen families strung out along this wooded peninsula jutting out into the sea. Comfortable, even beautiful houses they are, these houses, although, because of the isolation, always understaffed. So my doctor told me it would be good for me to hire myself out as an expensive Cordon Bleu jobbing cook. My doctor lived here himself, a poor bachelor, always hungry, so perhaps he had an interest in my cooking. "Go on, Anny," he said, with a smile. "Have a go."

Lynn Alloway is a beautiful woman, shamelessly beautiful. Shameless is a strange word to use, but it was the one I found myself using. Looking back, I see that I gazed at her through the eyes of a still very young woman nervously confronting her first experience of physical love. For I was in love then, deeply, painfully, engrossingly in love. I suppose what I am saying is that I felt a child before Lynn Alloway's woman. I did not feel a child before Ben. We crossed swords often, but I felt equal to him. Even when he was nagging me for my own good.

"Why don't you do it?" said Ben. "Go on, Anna, have a try."

"I'm too vain," I said.

"Why's that?"

"There I'd be, out in the kitchen, all hot and plain and in an apron, and there you would all be in your party clothes, smelling of Dior."

"I wouldn't smell of Dior."

"Chloroform, then."

"I haven't used that in years," he said. "We don't much now. About the cooking . . ."

"I'll think about it."

"You'll take my advice, Anny."

"Why will I?"

"Because it's good advice. And because I love you."

And he did love me. Only not sexually, but in a calm, quiet, best-friend kind of way. Because I have a large scar across my face and it is not easy for a man to fall in love with me. Not all across my face, you understand, only on my left cheek. When I turn my head you cannot see it.

The Alloway house is nearest to the sea, on a little wooded headland all its own. A narrow path winds down to the sea. It feels incredibly remote, although we are so close to London. Tim Alloway worked there and drove in every day. He was an industrialist and headed a complex of factories in a smoky London suburb near the Thames. I believe his own offices were behind Park Lane. This little house in the woods, a cottage really, but of an elegant sort, was their rented summer home. About a mile from the Alloways lived the Comptons, always jolly the Comptons. To the east and farthest away from the sea and nearest London were the Drivers, who were very rich. Dr. Ben Drummond lived close to the road. My house was about a hundred yards from him, we were neighbours. And then on the crown of the hill, but protected by its own lovely trees, is St. John's. Beautiful, famous St. John's. St. John's with its lovely curving Regency facade was the oldest and grandest house. In front of St. John's stood a pair of fine wrought iron gates, tall and slender, fit for a palace. They had been created by a local blacksmith over two hundred years ago, and contained in their design a delicate Fleur-de-lys, the golden lily of France, which was part of the Despenser coat of arms. Behind this great gate St. John's was empty. The Despensers, father and son, were away.

St. John's is an elegant, illustrious house but there is a secret flaw at the heart of it that you would not know unless told. Eighty years ago there was a fire, and half of the lovely house burned away. The owner loved it so much that he rebuilt the lost wing exactly to match the old as it had been. The plans still exist. Everything was reproduced with great craftsmanship, but it is no longer truly old. There is a great hidden wound in the old house. I often think it is just like me. Perhaps that is why I have such an affection for it.

And for a time it was my home. Old Mrs. Despenser had been a great influence in my life. I suppose you could say she had brought me up in her grande dame way. That is, she never did anything practical for me, but she always knew how to arrange for it to be done. When my teeth needed correction she saw I was taken to the best orthodontist in London. She chose my first dancing class, although she never sat there and watched me pirouette on one toe. She formed my manners, directing me with no more than a frown or a smile. Perhaps I was a responsive child, certainly she was a masterful woman. She left me a pearl necklace when she died, a necklace of gleaming white pearls too priceless to be worn.

I had been cooking around for six months. There was an initial reluctance on the part of my customers. They were a bit shy.

"I shall feel awkward," said Jean Driver, when I first sent out my cards. "You out in the kitchen and us eating your food. I mean, we've so often eaten your food at your table."

"So you know it's good."

"It's good all right . . . that peach flambée, you couldn't tell me how . . ." She lingered hopefully.

"No." I never gave away my recipes. Not if they were my own. What's in a book anyone can have. Anyway they can all read, even Jean Driver, who spent all her life in Bermuda before she came here and never learned how to tie her own shoelaces.

"I shall feel awkward," persisted Jean, "when I pay."

"No, you won't, Jean. Promise." I smiled.

The initial awkwardness soon wore off under the impact of my high charges. I've often noticed that you soon cease to think of a person as a servant or an inferior if you are paying them a good deal of money. It's a simple fact of human nature. I was giving them a luxury service and they were paying for it. I was a luxury object and my clients knew all about luxury objects.

I always said I wasn't doing it for the money, and in a way this was true, although I certainly enjoyed receiving it. I was paid in cash, and I put the money in a great tin box, and I supposed I might buy a mink coat from it one day.

I even invented a new sweetmeat, frangipani balls I called it, after an old recipe. I made it up in little bags, fastened with golden ribbons. It made little presents to give to friends and children.

It was a strange season. The early heat seemed to have brought with it a lot of sickness. The editor of the local paper had chicken-pox. Our postman had a heart attack while cutting his lawn. And a belt of great elms stretching across the sky-line sickened and died. Even the trees were ill.

Lynn Alloway and her Tim had rented the cedar cottage down by the sea from the Comptons for the summer. The Comptons always let this little cottage. The Alloways moved in early one morning in May, and on the next Sunday I went to cook for them. Lynn came out on to the small terrace to meet me, taller than me and golden with sun tan. Tim didn't appear then.

"Lovely of you to come early," she said. "You've got all the stuff with you?"

"I marketed this morning."

11

"I got in the extra cream. Also the unsalted butter."
She spoke appreciatively, as if she enjoyed food. "Every-
one says you're absolutely marvellous. I can't wait to eat.
Won't you come in after and have a drink with us?"

"I'll be busy clearing up." I had planned a long quiet
walk home past St. John's. I didn't really want to bother
with Lynn Alloway and her friends.

A bee flew out of the lavender bush and on to her arm.
With a neat chop from the side of her hand Lynn killed
it. Well, that didn't cost you anything, I thought. I'm glad
that wasn't me on your arm.

She walked me into the kitchen, where she had everything neatly laid out.

"I know my way round," I said, checking up with my
eyes. "I was often here with the Brands."

"Oh yes, they were the people here before us, weren't
they? I'd like to have met her. I heard she had some
marvellous jewels. Emeralds."

"She didn't really wear them," I said. "She kept them
in the bank. She wore costume jewellery like the rest
of us."

"Oh, I couldn't do that. I wear everything I've got."
She walked round the table. "Here's the butter. Here's
the asparagus for the flan. Did you know that asparagus
used to be thought of as an aphrodisiac?" She giggled.

"No." I didn't know it now, I thought she was just
talking for effect. "Thanks for the butter. You need fresh
butter and ice-water for pâté brisé."

"And the latter *you* can provide," I thought I heard
her say under her breath.

Later Tim Alloway came into the kitchen, walking
slowly.

"That was a very good boeuf à la mode," he said
politely. I don't think he really knew very much about
food and would probably have been just as happy with a
piece of nearly raw steak, burnt black on the outside and
very nearly alive in the middle. He was a simple man.
But, of course, simple men don't always have consistently
simple tastes, and in choosing Lynn as his wife he had
demonstrated this.

"Yes, it's an authentic dish," I said, a little priggishly I suppose, but I take cooking seriously.

"I've brought you a glass of brandy. Lynn said you wouldn't come in."

"I'll drink it with some coffee."

He put it on the table ready for me. I noticed the brandy he'd poured was in a fine glass and that he had placed it on a small silver tray. He had charming manners.

"You don't mind walking home alone?"

"No. Never."

"It still seems wrong to me to let a woman walk around on her own at night. I was brought up in a violent society, I suppose that's why." He didn't say where the society was, but I could think of a number of cities, countries, worlds that might qualify.

I was stacking the dishwasher as I spoke, although I wouldn't run it through, that was not part of my duties. But I left the kitchen orderly. I expected to find it tidy when I came, and I left it neat.

"Tim!" His wife's voice sounded from the terrace.

"Coming." He made the sort of face which said I regret to go but I must, and went back through the door.

I sat down and drank my brandy and coffee.

The sound of music and laughter floated in. They were all there, sitting on the little terrace. I was glad to be inside, apart from them. It wasn't a large party. The Comptons, and two people down from London, who would be driving back tonight. At least I took it they would be driving back. There was no great room, as far as I knew, in the little house.

I could hear Dolly Compton's voice. You nearly always can hear Dolly's voice if you are anywhere near. She has one of those voices that never fails to get its mark. As long as I could remember Jim Compton, her husband, had been groaning on and saying, Dolly, keep your voice down. She never did, though, and as the evenings wore on her voice would go higher and higher. She was at about mid-voice now.

I got up to go. A glance round the tidy kitchen satisfied me. I put my coat round my shoulders. I hadn't seen the guests from London arrive, but as I came up the path behind the terrace I could see them through the screen of roses and clematis. Nella Brand, Dolly Compton's cousin, had planted the roses. In spite of the fact that they came and went and only rented the cottage every summer, Nella still thought of it as very much her place. I did wonder why they had gone this time. There had been rumours that their marriage was ending. I wondered who'd get the emeralds? I often felt that the emeralds were the real things in their marriage and took the place of children for them.

I didn't mean to stare; I like my privacy, why shouldn't they like theirs? But they had a spotlight focussed on the chestnut tree above, and the light was reflected softly back at them as if they were on a stage. I suppose they were, in a way. Every single one of them was a natural actor.

Tim Alloway was talking to a woman who had her back to me. I couldn't see her face, only the top of her head over the back of the white garden chair. Tim was standing looking down at her. I could see his face well enough and he was looking at her with love. That he had delightful manners I had already discovered, perhaps he looked at all women that way.

Then I saw his lips silently frame one word: Darling.

I was just moving off, abashed. I hadn't meant and I hadn't been meant to see the word of love. Then I caught sight of Lynn Alloway. I don't know what *she* could see, possibly the expression on the other woman's face. On her own there was no expression at all. Her eyes were wide and round and empty, the muscles of her face slack.

For the moment she wasn't there. She had emptied herself away. But you had to ask where she had gone.

Tim Alloway turned and moved away. And Lynn moved, too, just a little. Why, she'll kill you, I thought.

There was a big red Mercedes parked in the road outside the cottage. I supposed it belonged to the visitors from London. I thought it would be a good idea if they got in it and drove back.

The road which runs through the woods is well lighted with pretty old-fashioned lamps, like iron lilies, bought up by Jim Compton when a London borough was changing over to more modern equipment. It's a private road, we pay for the upkeep ourselves, so the lighting goes off economically at midnight. But it was well before midnight, the moon was up, and the air was tranquil and warm.

By the time I had got to the curve of the road behind which stood St. John's, I heard a car coming up behind me. I stood on the grass to watch it pass. It was the red Mercedes.

This time I did not linger for a look at St. John's.

My green and purple parrot came floating down from the top of a picture as soon as I opened my front door. "You're not supposed to be out of your cage," I said.

"Ha, ha," he said. He always knew all the answers.

"How did you get out?"

"Bad boy," he observed.

"Yes, very bad boy." It was impossible to keep him locked up in his cage. He seemed able to open everything with that beak.

"Oh, Jackson," I said, scratching his wicked old head.

"Anny's back, Anny's back. Sweetheart," he said. You always had to remind yourself with Jackson that he couldn't really speak, that you weren't having a conversation with him, and that his responses meant no more to him than a trill to a canary. But sometimes, watching his bright alert eye, I did wonder.

I put Jackson back in his cage and covered it with a velvet cloth; he hated this and swore dreadfully when it appeared, but eventually he always fell asleep. He gave evidence sometimes of deeply resenting his bird nature, whose behaviour command he nevertheless had to obey.

I had settled myself in a pink cotton housecoat and was looking for something to read in bed, when the telephone rang. I stretched out my hand. I knew who it was.

"How did you get on with Lynn Alloway?"

"She thinks I'm frigid."

"Shame." I heard him chuckle. "Don't worry, it's not a medical condition. Not with you, anyway."

"Thank you."

"Do you like her, though?"

"Yes." I suddenly realised that I did. "I'm not sure if I'd want to work for her too much, though."

15

"Yes. She has that effect on a lot of people. And Tim? What about Tim?"

"Oh, a lovely man," I said.

"I'm not quite sure what to make of that."

"Well you've known him a long time. You must have noticed; he's irresistible."

"You *don't* like him."

"Perhaps I do. I feel I shouldn't, though. I think his wife's jealous of him."

"Oh no. You're wrong there. The boot's on the other foot. *He's* jealous."

"Ben," I said suddenly. "There was someone here again today."

"No, Anny, no." He said soothing.

"Jackson was out of his cage. I had it securely fastened."

"Not so securely as you thought. No one was there, Anny. I've explained. It's a symptom. A worry symptom."

"Melancholia I may have, crazy I am not."

"You don't have melancholia, Anny, or anything like it." He was short with me. "You had a very natural re-action to a period of great pain. It happens to everyone. Has the pain gone, by the way?"

"Yes."

"These feelings you have that someone is following you, that someone comes into your house when you are not well, they are subjective. They will pass, Anny, believe me."

"Ben, you are the only person I tell about these things. If you can't reassure me, who can?"

"Do you want me to come round?"

"No."

"There you are, then: you're stronger than you think."

And it was true. Funnily enough, these convictions I had that there was someone in the house or that there had been someone there, that I was being followed or had just ceased to be followed, did not frighten me. I took them calmly.

"You may be right," I said. My belief that someone was in the house was already fading. Perhaps the ease with which I always allowed him to reassure me meant something.

16

"You should believe me more, Anna. I give you good advice . . . You know why."

"Oh, is it one of your evenings for loving me, then?"

"You think nobody loves you."

"I think plenty of people love me. My aunt in Chester, even Jackson."

"You know what I mean."

I was silent. I refused to believe in his love.

"What about the farmer in Dodston who asked you to marry him? Didn't he love you?"

"He said so," I admitted.

"And you turned him down."

"He didn't want a wife. All he wanted was a good cook."

"He said he was going to emigrate, he was so upset."

"He looked perfectly happy at the Gladstow Horse Sales last week. And he's got an advertisement in the local paper for a working house-keeper."

Ben laughed. "You've got me beat. Sleep well. See you tomorrow."

"You might not," I said, but he was already gone. Probably I would see him tomorrow. Our lives seemed irreversibly bound together.

I went to sleep with my scarred cheek hidden in the pillow, as I always did. Yet it was the good side that had the pain. I have to wonder what part of the mind the pain comes from.

I didn't dream; I hardly ever do. To dream you have to be full of mystery, and I had none. I thought I saw my future plain.

I had half expected that Ben would visit me early the next day. I knew that he was, in a way, angry with me and that was a sort of punishment. He didn't put it that way to himself. He thought he was looking after me. Nevertheless, it was a punishment. If you are on the receiving end of a process, you know if what you are getting is a punishment or a favour, and I knew.

So I wasn't surprised to see him there on the doorstep, carrying my letters, a small box, and a bottle of milk.

"Lot of milk and cream you use for a girl your size," he said.

"I need it for cooking. I'm trying out a new recipe today."

I kept quiet. He and I got cross at each other often enough as it was without my showing irritation where no offence was meant. He probably did admire me as an intelligent cook.

"What are you making with all that cream and milk?"

"A cream pudding, an almond variation of crême brulée."

"And you never put on an ounce. Speaking as a student of human metabolism, I find that interesting."

"I don't eat all I cook. Mrs. Twining helps."

"And me. Have you got anything for me now? I was out on an early call."

"There is a little sweet-cured ham, I think."

"And some of your coffee? It's for your coffee I love you, really."

"I could teach you to make it yourself if you weren't so lazy."

"How sweetly you put it."

He ate hungrily, he always did. I often wondered what he lived on in that tumbled old house. I think he slept some nights in the room behind his surgery. I didn't blame him for not going home much. Since his father had died, the house had been empty. None of us had ever realised at the time how much he had filled it; and now Ben did not. Perhaps one day he would. Ben might amount to something considerable in time: I couldn't be sure. It was easy to believe he would be a great man. But easy now to believe he might fail. It's so terribly simple, isn't it, to fail to reach your true stature?

Physically, however, he had certainly reached it. But he was too thin, far too thin. And, in spite of the flower in his buttonhole, not thoughtful about his clothes or his appearance. He did not care. And he smoked too much, far too much.

After we'd eaten, we sat for a moment in silence. Then he said, I suppose to me, but certainly half to himself, "I'm a good doctor."

"I know you are."

"I lost a patient this morning, Anny."

"Dead, you mean?"

He hesitated. "Yes."

"I'm sorry. But it must happen all the time. It must have happened before."

"It upset me, that was all."

"Was it anyone special? A child? Someone you knew well?"

"No, an old man. He would have gone anyway, this year or next. I just wasn't ready for it today, somehow." He got up and moved restlessly round my little kitchen. "Today."

"There's nothing special about today that makes it no day for dying. There's never a day like that."

"No." He had the cover off the parrot's cage. The bird had been rustling round and grumbling for some time. Now it blinked in the light and looked fierce. "Hello, Jackson."

Jackson did not answer but banged his beak angrily at the bars of his cage. "He likes it in there, really," I said.

"Oh, sure. Don't we all like our cages."

I didn't answer.

"You haven't opened your post."

"No." I inspected the little pile. "I can see what it is. A bill. A letter from a girl I was at school with. Another bill."

"And the box?" He had picked it up and was inspecting it.

"Oh yes, the box. Well, it's a sort of bomb."

"What?"

"Don't worry. It's delayed action."

"What do you mean?"

"Open it and see."

Somewhat gingerly, he had believed my words more than he'd intended, he tore off the wrappings. "A rose. One single rose."

"Yes, that's it." I picked it out of the box and put it in a vase. "I get one a day."

"And which admirer sends them?"

"I don't think they're sent in love, somehow," I laughed.

Ben shook his head. "You're a funny girl. You get anxious about people following you and being in the house, which is just a worry symptom, but you take this daily gift of a rose with a laugh."

"What's a rose, after all? Only a flower."

"It would worry me."

"I'm not afraid of a flower." I put out my hand and stroked the petals, which were soft and cool.

All the same, I didn't like the daily arrival of the rose.

"But you're frightened of something, Anny," he said, watching my face. "If not of the rose, of something. What are you frightened of, Anny?"

Well, I was frightened of horses, thunderstorms, spiders, dark passages and love, among other things, but I preferred not to say so to him. I didn't want to talk about my fears. Everyone has their own set, custom-built for them, and I am no exception. Perhaps I have one or two extra, rather special fears, arisen from the circumstances I find myself in.

We were still there, standing together in my kitchen, when the telephone rang. I picked it up.

"Hello? Yes, he's here." I covered the mouthpiece. "For you. Mrs. Alloway."

"I left a list of my calls at the surgery so I could be reached in an emergency."

"She's an emergency," I said, handing him the telephone.

"Dr. Drummond speaking." He had his professional voice on. "Yes, I've got that. Yes. No, do nothing till I get there."

I stood waiting. For a moment I thought he wasn't going to say anything. Then he said, reluctantly, "It's Tim Alloway. He's ill."

"I thought he must be dying, from her voice."

"She thinks he may be. You'd better come with me. I may need some nursing help."

But he wasn't dying, of course, he was staggering around the sitting-room looking white and swearing. He leaned against a table when he saw us. "Bit weak in the legs, damn it," he said.

"I didn't expect to find you on them." Ben put his bag on the table. "Better sit down and let me have a look at you. From what your wife said, you were pretty bad."

20

"Feeling a bit better now," said Tim, but his skin looked greenish-white. "Thought I had a hangover at first. We did have a bit of a thing last night."

On your own then, I thought, for your friends from London left early.

"But God, it's never been like this." There was a line of sweat forming on his upper lip.

"Sit down." Ben pushed him gently into a chair and took his wrist between his finger, feeling the pulse. "Pain?"

"Yes."

"Sick?"

"The lot."

"Well, you'll have to get to bed, Tim, and let me examine you."

I sat down in a chair to wait. Presently Lynn Alloway appeared, and sat down. "Cigarette?"

"No, thank you."

"Well, I shall. I need one. What a night. I thought poppa had caught the last train out last night, all right. He kept me so busy I didn't dare leave him, even to ring the doctor." Her hand holding the cigarette shook. "It was instant illness. One minute he was all right, and the next he was having these terrible pains."

"And being sick?"

"That came later."

I saw her look at me thoughtfully. "He was all right earlier in the evening. You didn't notice anything, did you?"

"No."

"You know, I believe he ate something that didn't agree with him." Her eyes rested speculatively on me.

"The food must have been all right," I said. "You all ate it, too."

"Yes," she agreed, nodding her head. There were a few faint sounds drifting in from the room down the corridor where Tim Alloway and Ben were. I could hear Ben's voice. Not what he was saying, but just his tones. He had a nice voice. I couldn't hear Tim's voice, but I could hear him coughing.

"You know what he said to me?" Lynn spoke suddenly. "Last night when he asked me to pour some whisky.—

21

Hand me my poison. That's exactly what he said. Hand me my poison."

And I bet you did, I thought.

Ben came back into the room. "He ought to rest. I've told him to go to bed. I think he's over the worst by now." He looked worried. There was an unusual stiffness in his manner.

"But what is it?" said Lynn.

"I'm not quite sure yet." Ben looked even more worried. "I'm watching him."

"Is there anything I am to do?"

"Keep him quiet. See he drinks a lot. He won't want to eat, I expect."

"Are you going to prescribe anything?"

"Yes." He had been writing on a small pad. "Can you get this made up?"

"I'll take it down to the village," I said. "I'll drive that way, and the shop will deliver it."

"I'll go and sit with Tim, then."

"I should let him sleep," said Ben. "He's tired."

"I don't like to think of him alone."

"You can look in occasionally."

Lynn Alloway saw us to the door. Her eyes met mine and then flicked away nervously. She didn't want me to look at her, and it seemed something more than the natural vanity of a beautiful woman who knew she wasn't looking her best. You look self-conscious, even guilty, I thought. I dismissed the thought, but it came back, and I shivered. That's one of the things about guilt, it spreads outward touching more and more people.

"You'll come back?"

"Certainly." Ben relaxed his stiffness. "Buck up, Lynn, he's going to be all right."

"Is he?"

We got into Ben's car without speaking. He drove off silently. Poor old Ben, I thought. He's got a hot potato here, all right.

"You'll get the medicine, Anny?"

"Of course."

He nodded without answering, driving carefully along

22

the curving road to my house. St. John's lay above us, behind its woods. I could just see a chimney.

"What's the matter with him?"

"Oh, gastric upset of some sort. Virus infection. Spoiled food. I'm not sure which yet."

"She's poisoned him."

"No, Anny, no."

"Yes. What's more, you think so yourself."

"I haven't said so." He was annoyed.

"You didn't need to. Gastric infection, spoiled food. That's not the way you talk."

"Stop it, Anny."

"You hadn't forgotten that I cooked the dinner he ate?"

"No, I hadn't forgotten."

"I don't like it."

"Anny, what is the matter with you? You keep inventing fictions, fables. They're just cover-up worries for something else. What is on your mind?"

We had arrived at my house, and it was just as well. I got out of the car and slammed the door. After all, we had ended on a note of anger.

Music was pouring through my house as I walked in. Mrs. Twining, who cleans my house twice a week from top to bottom, loves music and assures me that she works best to it. So she has permission to use my record player as she polishes. She is eclectic and discriminating in her choice of music. Yesterday the Beatles, tomorrow Beethoven. Today it was Mozart. The Countess's lament from *The Marriage of Figaro*. The sound was glorious, full of ease, but the singer had died tragically in a car crash a year before. The car had hit a tanker full of petrol and she had burnt to a cinder. Nothing, nothing had been left of her at all. And now that dead voice was ringing through my room. I went over and switched off the machine.

"She sings that beautifully, doesn't she?" said Mrs. Twining, appearing at the door.

"But she's dead," I said.

Mrs. Twining looked surprised. She didn't say anything but I could see the words "And so's Mozart" written on her face.

"I'm sorry," I apologised. "I know it's irrational of me."

"No, not what I'd call irrational, exactly," said Mrs. Twining. "More, well, *primitive*. And you're *not* primitive."

"I try not to be."

"There's a tribe in the middle of Africa that fears any relic of the dead. These people think the dead are malevolent." Mrs. Twining studied anthropology in her spare time, as well as music.

"I don't think the dead are evil," I said.

"Of course, all those big books on anthropology are terribly out of date. I dare say that tribe are all sitting round their television sets now, watching commercials." She laughed cheerfully.

I laughed too.

"That's better," said Mrs. Twining, "You looked quite white. Shall I get you a cup of coffee? I expect your blood sugar needs a boost."

Last year Mrs. Twining had studied psychology, and believed that the body influenced the mind.

She moved efficiently round the kitchen, preparing the drink. She was as good a cook as I was, but in a completely different style. I think I'd call her a "Round the World in Thirty Days" cook, or Anyone who can Read can Cook. Hawaiian strüdel or East Anglian bouillabaisse, it was all one to her, she tried them all. And because she was a naturally good cook, they turned out well.

"I was up at St. John's yesterday, helping Mrs. Franks give a dust round. My word, it's a lovely house. I've never been in it before. Outside, yes, to see the gardens, but never inside. They're coming back, you know."

I was sceptical. Mrs. Twining made a point of being first with the news, sometimes to the sacrifice of accuracy. On the other hand, she had a flair; it didn't do to underrate her.

"Or that's the signal." Mrs. Twining had served in the Wrens during the war, and naval slang occasionally appeared in her conversation. "But then they often send that signal, don't they, and then don't come?"

"It has happened," I agreed.

"Twice before, Mrs. Franks says."

"Well, she doesn't mind, does she?"

"No. Rather likes it. She's such a lazy old cow. Less work to do with no one there."

I made a deprecating noise.

"Oh, it's all right for you. You see the best side of her. Of course, she's getting on. I dare say she does find the work harder than she did. Six in staff they used to be up there, she says, and three of them in the house-keeper's room. Must have been quite old-fashioned."

"They did keep up a certain amount of state," I said.

"Those days are over," said Mrs. Twining, with gusto.

Don't you believe it, I thought. The pattern of spending has changed, that's all. Look at the Drivers. The Drivers were truly rich but they lived very simply. You knew they were rich because nothing about them was ever old or dirty or worn. Everything was always fresh and new and sweet, from the flowers in Jean's bedroom to the thick towels in the bathroom. Aged furniture they had, but it had been made in eighteenth-century work-rooms by great craftsmen and lovingly cared for ever since. Unobtrusively, civilisation was constantly renewing itself around the Drivers, and this was what it was like to be rich in the mid-twentieth century.

"Oh, I forgot to tell you old Lady Madden was looking for you."

"I wonder what she wants." Biddy Madden (she was indeed the widow of a knight, although, God knew, one would hardly guess it) was an elderly neighbour. There was more to our relationship by now than mere contiguity. I saw the despair in her, and she knew I did.

"Knowing her, I should say it was a loan. You usually do give her one about now, don't you? I don't know why you let her get away with it."

"I don't really let her get away with it," I said uneasily. "I feel sorry for her, she's been all at sixes and sevens since she lost her grandson. She wasn't too bad till then."

"She always drank," said Mrs. Twining firmly. "Always. You used to be able to smell the brandy on her breath. It's come down to rum now. Mind you, he wasn't a good boy, as I remember. She's better off without him."

"Perhaps she doesn't think so. Anyway, it's not only the boy."

"You mean the girl too?" said Mrs. Twining. "The one that ran away? That was before I came to work for you."

"No, she didn't run away." I knew this, even if I didn't know anything else about Lily Madden's departure. Only carefully prepared sentences by my seniors had been passed down to me about Lily. "Sick, my dear, not herself at all" or "She's gone away for a course of treatment," such were the phrases taught to me. Only as I grew up had I formed them into the starker truth that Lily was in a Geneva nursing home for something more than a rest cure. Mad. Even now I never said it aloud. "She's ill," I said to Mrs. Twining, daring her to ask another question.

"I think we'll have a bit of Beethoven," said Mrs. Twining, "I don't think that coffee's done you as much good as I thought. And you can't feel sorry for yourself when you listen to that man's music."

She went through to my sitting-room and soon the Beethoven Violin Concerto was calling confidently through the house. I heard her singing to the music as she polished.

I saw her just as she had her coat on ready to depart. I was off to the village to collect the medicine for Tim Alloway. She accepted my offer of a lift and sat without talking throughout the short drive.

"You know, you don't want to worry too much," she said suddenly, as she got out. "You're a lovely girl."

I moved the driving mirror so I could see the curve of my cheek, the faint shadow under my eye. The right side. My best side. The side without a mark.

I had to wait a few minutes for Tim Alloway's bottle of medicine to be wrapped. I saw Dolly Compton from the shop window, she was shopping. When I got back with the medicine, which looked like a bottle of nothing (a dab of peppermint and chalk, I suspected), Tim Alloway had been violently sick. He was lying back on a chaise longue, looking white and drawn and complaining about feeling cold.

"You ought to be in bed," I said, handing over the bottle from the chemist's.

"I'm going." He heaved himself up. "Oh God, my legs *ache*."

"Any other symptoms?"

"That'll do to be going on with."

"You must have some other symptoms."

"Here, what is this?" He leaned against the doorpost for support, and groaned. "Don't come near me. I've got a fire alight inside me."

I stayed until he was in bed and Lynn Alloway had telephoned Ben again and I could hear Ben's car arriving. Then I walked through to the kitchen and made myself at home.

I wanted a good look around, and I thought they would all be too busy to notice me for a time. I looked in the refrigerator to see if there were any remains of the food I had cooked for the dinner last night. A little of the cream pudding had been left and some of the vichyssoise soup. The refrigerator looked remarkably bare, as if someone had made a clean sweep of it. Indeed, there was nothing in it, except some eggs and two unopened bottles of milk.

I had a quick prowl round the kitchen. I had left it clean, and it was still clean. No cooking had been done in the Alloway household that morning. This was about what I would have expected. Lynn Alloway didn't look like a keen cook or a big breakfast eater, and Tim of course hadn't been up to it. I looked in the coffee pot. Someone had drunk a little black coffee that morning. I tasted it. A Java and Kenya coffee mix, lightly roasted. Last night I had made a pot of Mocha coffee. So someone had made this brew freshly this morning. The coffee tasted bitter on my lips. Although I had had hardly any in my mouth, I went over to the sink and rinsed my mouth out with water.

Then I continued my investigation of the kitchen. At the end of ten minutes I had found nothing of interest. Everything in the kitchen was either tinned, dried, or frozen solid.

So I went quietly back into the hall and closed the door behind me. I could hear voices from behind a door. I judged that Ben was asking questions and Lynn Alloway was answering them. And not making much of a job of it, either, judging by the extreme shortness of her replies and the long angry rumble of Ben's voice. I knew his voice always got deeper when he was angry, unlike my own, which rose. It would have been interesting to have listened to them, and I probably would have done so, if they had not then appeared.

I thought Ben wasn't too pleased to see me there again. A flicker of displeasure came into his eyes before he slipped his professional mask back on. Ben really had a natural poker face, which must have been useful to him in his work.

"Hello, Anna," he said curtly. You here again, was what he meant.

"She brought the medicine," said Lynn.

"What did you do with it?"

I looked around. "I gave it to Tim. I think it's still on the table. He didn't take any. I don't think it would have done him much good."

"I'm trying something else now."

Yes, I thought to myself. Why not? You keep trying, because I cooked the meal and I'd like Tim Alloway alive and well.

Ben turned to Lynn. "I'll do some tests. Try to put down exactly what is causing all this. But I think what I've given him should help."

"He was nearly asleep when we left."

"Sleep is what he needs."

I thought Ben wasn't behaving at all naturally, he seemed almost a parody of a doctor. He must have been rigid with anxiety. I wondered Lynn Alloway couldn't sense it.

"Is there any of the food he had yesterday left?" said Ben.

I waited to see what she answered.

"I don't think so," said Lynn Alloway vaguely. "No, I don't think so. Why?"

"I could have tested it."

"I cooked it," I said. "It was perfectly wholesome."

"We all ate it," said Lynn. "I didn't have some of everything, but each dish was tasted by someone. We had guests to dinner. The Comptons and some London friends."

"And are they all right?"

"The Comptons are," I said.

"So that leaves your other friends. Can you telephone them?"

"Yes." She was reluctant, though.

"Do it now."

"I believe we'd have heard if they were unwell," she said, as she moved slowly towards the telephone.

"Try, all the same."

She dialled. I could hear the number ringing out. "No answer," she said, with relief.

"Let me try. Give me the number." Ben spun the number out efficiently. In no time at all a voice answered. Silently he handed the telephone to Lynn.

I walked out into the garden and got into my car. I didn't want to stay and listen while Lynn spoke to the woman at whom Tim had looked with love. However Lynn spoke, whatever she said, there would be lies and murder in her voice. It was such a lovely voice, too. I couldn't help thinking that in other circumstances it would be a pleasure to listen to her.

I had to wait some time, but eventually Ben came out. He saw me in the car and walked over. "Well?" I said.

"The other people are all right."

We looked at each other silently. "What did you give him?" I said.

"Nothing specific."

"You mean you haven't made a diagnosis?"

"I mean I gave him narcotics to help the pain, and I told Lynn to give him ice to help the vomiting and control the thirst."

"He ought to be in the hospital."

"I'm getting a nurse to help Lynn."

"Good. Who?"

"Does it matter to you, Anna?"

"It matters a lot. I cooked the last meal he ate."

"Mrs. Knolly's going to look in."

"She's a layer-out, not a nurse," I said.

"Anna!"

"However, she'll do as a witness."

"A witness?"

"I don't want to be accused of killing anyone."

"He's not going to die, Anna."

I looked down the road. "There's Mrs. Knolly's car now. She must have set out as soon as you rang her."

"Good, I must get in. You go home now, Anna. Have a rest." He patted my shoulder and went back into the house.

I passed Mrs. Knolly as I drove away, and waved. She didn't take her hands off the wheel, but just nodded. It was a miracle she could drive at all, really, her long-distance vision was shocking. She was a better nurse than I had implied to Ben, but I knew he would have chosen her in any case, tied as she was to him by custom and old associations.

I drove home by way of St. John's. I wanted a refresher course in the humanities, and St. John's had always provided this for me. It was a beautiful house, you felt you were linked with an older quieter world when you looked at it.

There it stood among its trees and gardens, graceful and elegant and empty. It was a pity it had to be empty, I didn't like it empty, but for the moment that was the way it had to be. Mrs. Franks thought the Despensers were coming back for a visit, but they wouldn't come. I knew they wouldn't come.

Jackson was in his cage when I got home; I opened it for him, but he was sulky and would not move. Even his feathers looked an angry purple and green.

"So you don't want to leave your cage, Jackson?" I said, scratching his head, which remained rigid, fixed in his displeasure. "You've discovered it's got its virtues. So it has. It's safe, protected and quiet. Move over, Jackson, and let me get in there with you."

Ben gave me twenty-four hours off, during which I ordered some new clothes for the summer, had my hair washed, and cooked dinner for Jean Driver, before he brought his problems to me.

He came in, without making any pretence of just happening to be passing this way, or wanting some breakfast, and slumped in a chair. Whether he knew it or not, he took the same chair whenever he was in a bad mood.

"Well, what is it?"

"It was poison, Anny." He was staring glumly out of the window. "Tim Alloway had about two grains of arsenic through him."

"Is that a lot?"

"Enough to kill him. I don't know why it didn't, really. Unless it was that rich dinner you cooked for him." He looked away from the window and smiled at me.

So lobster bisque and boeuf à la mode and strawberries en surprise had worked to save Tim's life. Lynn Alloway wasn't going to like that very much, if she ever realised it.

"I don't know what I'm going to do about it."

"Who have you told?"

"Just you, Anny."

"You have to tell Tim Alloway."

He grimaced. "I'd like to avoid telling anyone. I'd like to bury it for ever."

"You can't do that."

"You don't know everything, Anny." He was looking out of the window again. "I wish I knew what to do." He looked very young and sorry for himself. "Anyway, I won't do anything yet. Tim is getting better, I can leave it for a while."

"I should just say a word to Lynn Alloway. Tell her to watch what her husband eats. That'll slow her down. For a while."

"Don't ever say that sort of thing aloud. Any time. Anywhere."

He got up to go. "I feel better now. Thanks, Anna. Have you got a cup of coffee? And any of the chocolate cake?"

"So early in the morning?"

"I can always eat that cake."

I cut him a slice of gâteau négresse and poured some coffee. He must have added to my food bills considerably.

"It's a sort of ganache."

He finished the last crumbs of chocolate cake and kissed me goodbye. "Look after yourself, Anna. You're a bit too thin. I see St. John's is opened up again."

31

"I think Mrs. Franks is giving it a clean," I said.

"No, not Mrs. Franks. The Despensers are back. I saw the boy in the woods this morning. Makes you think a bit, doesn't it?"

2

Ben and I were very close; but all the same, we didn't tell each other everything, and when we did tell things, then, sometimes, it was not always for the reason that we pretended. That is, we were passing a message to each other, but its words were not always what it meant.

Now I wondered what Ben was *really* telling me. That the Despensers were back? Yes, certainly his message contained hard information: true, too, no doubt. That the Despensers were back and he, Ben, found this fact surprising? There was an element of this in his statement. Yes, but I thought he wanted me to know that he understood I'd be surprised too. And this *did* give me pause for thought.

The first thing to do, of course, was to find out if the Despensers were indeed back home. I could hardly believe it, but I had never known Ben to tell me something that was demonstrably untrue. And I hoped he had never found me out in a falsehood, either. But of that I couldn't be sure. We had known each other a long, long time, since childhood and upward, and who could say if in that time I had not misled him?

I put Jackson back in his cage and walked out of my house. Where I live the ground slopes away into a small hollow. It's very secluded and quiet. A great main road, heavy with traffic to the city, circles the base of our peninsula, hidden in a thick belt of trees. You would hardly know it was there: there is little sound to betray it, only an absence of birds, and occasionally, when the wind is in the right direction, on a summer evening, a thin smell of diesel oil.

There are so many trees here to protect us, but, of course, they are our trees. We pay for them and preserve them, they are not public trees, you will never find families picnicking in our woods. We live on our secluded peninsula, surrounded and protected by our paid-for trees. They even bloom when we want them to, because among them we have caused to be planted trees that flower at different stages through the year. These trees, adult trees (because after all infant trees would not be tall enough to guard us) were torn from their matrix and brought here in their prime. If they got too big, or misshapen, or if we just didn't happen to like the colour, we would get rid of them. But we paid a good price for them. Money was our forester.

I walked up the rise in the road, putting my house behind me, and striking up through the belt of chestnut trees towards St. John's.

I saw him almost at once as he walked through the trees alone. I halted for a moment to observe him. He'd grown since I saw him last. At his age, sixteen, that was still possible. Probably he would be a tall man like his father in the end.

"Hello, Peter," I said.

He saw me, of course, but he pretended not to. Or was it just a pretence? One of the worries about him had always been the way he would withdraw into a world of his own. In a less talented child it could have been near psychotic. It was hardly true to call him a child now, either. The face was thin; the eyes looked as though they had seen a little too much of something disquieting.

"Hello."

"I thought you hadn't seen me."

"I did and I didn't. I saw you, but you didn't fit in with what I was thinking, so your face didn't seem to match you, somehow. Now, it does. You've come together."

"I didn't expect you back home yet."

He didn't answer that one, didn't like it, perhaps, or he may have thought I was being tactless.

"But it's nice to see you again," I persevered. "And your father, too, is he back?"

"He's in London." He amplified this. "Today. Back tonight."

"Are you on your own?"

"I don't mind."

He might have said: "I'm always on my own."

"Anyway, I love these woods," he said.

"Yes, I love them too." I looked up at the rich thickness of leaves meeting above us. It always smelt cool and sweet in the woods.

"They're called Ironwood in the old maps, did you know that? Ironwood. It's a good name, isn't it? It's because they used to do primitive iron smelting here in tiny forges, with charcoal from the trees. Do you remember we found the remains of an old forge here once?"

"I remember."

"It probably dated back to the seventeenth century. I was only a kid when we found it. I'd be able to do a better job on the dating now."

"Yes. I expect you would."

Possibly he felt he'd been abrupt. "I've been at school in Paris, you know," he said. "My French is quite good now." Then he smiled: he was his father's son after all, and knew how to exercise charm. "I learnt a lot of French history. Not much else." His smile went away. "So when we go into the Common Market I shall at least be able to get a job as a courier or a commercial traveller. I must do something."

So his future worried him, and perhaps his past too. It must be like peering into an abyss.

"I think now and I've always thought," I said deliberately, "that your father made a mistake in taking you away."

"You mean you were on my side?" He gave me a careful look.

"Yes."

35

"No one was on my side," he said. "No one. Because no one believed what I said."

"I believed you," I said. But there was a reservation in my voice, and he heard it.

"Yes, my father believed me. He said, I'm your father and I believe you. But he took me away, well away. And he said, don't let's talk about it, don't let's ever talk about it. That's how he believed me."

"That was three years ago," I said slowly. "Would it help if I said I believe you *now?*"

"It's too late now." It was terrible to hear the adult note in his voice. "Now it's too late. I don't know what to believe myself any longer, and that's what really counts."

And then with one of those sudden changes of mood that were characteristic of him, he said, "Oh, Anna, there's a waxwing in the wood. That's terribly unusual at this time of the year. They're only visitors, you know, and usually clear off when the berries are over. This one must have stayed behind."

"Perhaps it got lost."

"It's a passerine, you know. That means percher. It perches."

"Don't most birds?"

"Passerines are the largest order of birds," he said, continuing the flow of information. "The name comes from their toes, three outward and one forward, so that they can hang on a branch. You have to find a name for birds, somehow. All the song birds are passerines."

"I wonder what parrots are? You couldn't really call them song birds, could you, but they certainly perch?"

"It's a psittaciform," he said at once. "That's easy, you can get the disease psittacosis from it. It's a wasting disease."

"Jackson's in good health. He's not wasting away."

"Oh, have you got a parrot? Can I come and see it?"

"If your father says so," I said.

"Oh, he'll say so. He thinks a lot of you."

"Does he? We don't always agree." This was, in fact, a very restrained way of putting it; we had had some notable quarrels.

"He's always polite when he speaks about you, though," observed his son. "And he isn't about everybody."

"I can believe that." And so I could. I knew, at first hand, the sharpness of Neil Despenser's tongue.

"I expect he'll want to see you when he gets back from London."

"No, I don't think so."

"No?" He sounded puzzled. And then he was off again, at a new tangent. "St. John's is going to be repainted. Outside, anyway. I don't know what we're doing about the inside."

St. John's was opened to the public once a week, in spring and summer. Not a lot of people came. After all, it was not one of the great show places like Blenheim Palace or Woburn Abbey, but every Thursday during the season visitors trickled in, to wander round the gardens, through the gold drawing room, and to end up in the library to look at the small and suspect Titian and the large and authentic Sisley. My own favourite picture was a tiny little Berthe Morisot of a girl who looked like Cléo de Mérode. Knowing the family, I have always thought it probably was a portrait of that celebrated lady. The library also had paintings of historical interest but of a rather bizarre nature. Most of them were portraits, real or imagined, I was never quite sure which, of famous murderers. These had been collected by Neil Despenser's grandfather, who had been keenly interested in criminology. He had a good collection of books on the subject, as well as pictures. Dr. Palmer's face leered down at you above a row of Notable British Trials, and Madeleine Smith faced Florence Maybrick over a row of books on Jack the Ripper. I regret to say that, as children, this was always our most frequented part of the library. Ben and I, and in his turn Peter, were keen students of the details of crimes and knew that Dr. Palmer of Rugeley poisoned about fifteen people and was twenty-five when he poisoned his mother-in-law and thirty when he was hanged. We knew that Florence Maybrick kept poison in her hat-box and that Lizzie Borden was very fond of mutton. We had looked at a picture of the sleepy Worcestershire town where Madeline Pollock had lived and studied a map of it. At one time we played Murder Games, albeit of an intellectual kind. Mary Stuart, Darnley and Rizzio. Charlotte Corday and Marat. Looking back, I saw that imagination and sex were about equally involved in it. I was always the murderer, never the victim. I had never thought about that until now.

"It's lovely that way, it is." The ordered beauty inside St. John's never varied, it was always a pleasure to see. It had been a joy to me all the time I was growing up. I was fortunate to have lived in its ambience.

"Yes." He smiled at me warmly. "I think so. I still think of it as my home, you know. That's funny, isn't it, when I'm hardly ever there? The apartment in Paris is nice. That's home, too."

"Is it?" I felt suddenly sad and tired.

"Yes. When I come in from school in the afternoon and it's warm and full of sun and smells of that sort of beeswax polish on the furniture, then it's home."

He'd been away too long, I thought, ever to settle down at St. John's again. Perhaps it was just as well.

He punctured my mood again with his parting comment. "Do you still make that fab honey cake? Can I come and have a slice?"

"Any time you say, I've got one in the tin now." I hadn't, but I would go away and bake one.

I watched him walk off through the trees. He went away walking smartly, but very soon he was staring up at the trees, occasionally stopping. I guessed he had started off on another topic and had already forgotten me.

But I couldn't forget him so easily, and I trudged back home feeling miserable. What terrible things we do to people, especially children, when we try to help them. All of us, from his father to Ben Drummond, had acted with the very best of intentions towards Peter, and I hadn't the least doubt in the world that we had done him harm. We had put a sharp knife right down his middle, and cut him in two. All his life he would feel the effects of it.

The usual rose had arrived when I got back home. A little late today. I put it in a silver bowl, where it joined its predecessors of the week, all six of them. I found they

38

usually lasted a week, so, except on Bank Holiday and so on, which threw deliveries out a bit, I usually had a bowl of roses. Today, for the first time, it occurred to me that this had always been meant.

I telephoned Ben late that afternoon.

"Yes, I've seen Peter," I said.

"How is he?"

"Much the same," I said.

"How is he?"

"Changing. Growing up. We didn't do him a service, you and I, when we advised his father to take him away."

"It was hardly advice. You don't advise Neil Despenser. Just a word."

"He's sensitive where the boy's concerned."

"Of course. Still, he was better out of the country."

I was silent.

"Anna, it could have come to a police prosecution."

"He was thirteen," I said. "Barely thirteen."

"Twelve is the age of criminal responsibility in this country."

"God, I hate you sometimes," I said.

"Yes, I know."

"There won't be any trouble now, will there?"

"I don't suppose for a minute Neil Despenser would have been back if he'd thought *that* likely."

"It's the house, you see," I said. "They do love St. John's. He may just have wanted to see it."

"No one loves a house that much."

"I'm not sure if he doesn't," I said.

"We shall have to burn it down again, then," he said lightly. "Someone had a try once, didn't they, and never succeeded?"

"I've often thought of doing it," I said. There was a pause. While he was working things out, I knew he must be puzzled. He didn't like what I had said.

"Don't get too involved, will you?" he said. "They're tough, that family, the Despensers. In the end, they survive."

I could hear clicks on the telephone line.

"I'd better get off the line now, someone is trying to

reach one of us. Probably it's Jean, for me. I know she wants me to do a dinner for her."

"Yes, I know. I'm going."

But the telephone remained quiet for the rest of the day. It must have been a call for Ben coming through. I hoped it was a personal call. I liked to think he had a life outside our little group.

I settled down to checking a few biscuit recipes for my own amusement. I was making a dictionary of recipes. It's amazing how many began with almond: almond chicken, almond cream, almond shortbread. I was lost in a dream of candied peel and almonds and egg whites and cherries when Jackson interrupted me. True to form, he had nothing original to say. "He's a good boy," he said gloomily. He never sounded happy, why should he? He was fidgeting around in his cage, but making no attempt to get out. "He's a good boy." He was a consistent performer, always getting the intonation and enunciation exactly the same.

But I was beginning to know him, and I understood that he had heard something I could not hear. I sat and worked. Presently a car drove up fast and stopped, quickly yet smoothly. I could guess who arrived like that.

"Anna? Anna?"

I went to the door and opened it. "Come in, Lynn," I watched her approach. "The door's always unlocked, you know."

"I didn't want to come in unless I knew you were here, because of that wretched bird. He swore at me last time I came in."

"Jackson doesn't swear."

"For me, he does." She was wearing trousers and her own blonde hair. Last night's Renaissance confusion had obviously been a wig. "I take it you've heard the news about Tim?"

There could only be one subject between us two at the moment: her husband. I had cooked for him and she had lived with him.

"Oh, come on," she said impatiently. "You know. One way or another, you *know*."

Her voice rose, and, perhaps in response, Jackson made a clucking, deprecating noise.

"Shut up, darling," she said absently. "Look," she said, "I'm a wife whose husband has nearly been poisoned. Arsenic. And you've got to think about your position, too. You cooked the last meal he ate." She lit a cigarette. "That's why I've come. We've got to talk."

Jackson did swear then. Two or three words I was surprised he knew.

"There you are, you see. That bird doesn't like me." She looked round for an ashtray. I had already noticed that she was a woman careful of her own property, and of other people's. She would not drop ash on my floor. I got her a little Wedgewood saucer for the cigarettes. "That's really too pretty to use," she said. "That's a nice rug. Shiraz, isn't it? You ought to look after it. You haven't got a cup of coffee, have you? You make beautiful coffee, and I could certainly drink one." She pushed at her heavy gold hair.

"You don't think it might poison you?" But I got up.

"Oh, don't be silly. You do that to me, and we don't either of us have any problems, do we?"

She put down her cigarette. "I'll know who did it and you'll know I know and I promise I'll see plenty of other people know. No, you and I are in trouble because nothing is quite as certain as that. You think I gave it to him. You do, don't you? But you're not quite sure. I'm not sure about you."

"Why did you really come to see me?"

"I'm not sure, really. For consolation? Or just to check up on you? Perhaps I want you to cook me another meal? I think I did have that in my mind."

"I'll do that for you. Any time you like."

"Yes." She took out another cigarette. "I don't know what's the matter today. All these cigarettes taste awful. What about that coffee?"

She was still sitting there when I got back with a pot of coffee.

"I've thought of what I wanted to say to you," she said. "You think I came round here to accuse you? Oh, don't

41

look like that. I know you did think so. But I didn't. I came here to warn you."

"Warn me?"

"Yes." She drank the coffee I had poured out. "Well, I suppose you could call it warn. You could be in a dangerous position."

"That sounds more like a threat than a warning."

"No, it isn't. Really it isn't. Just think about yourself. This is a funny little neck of the woods. I don't know what you think about yourself."

"I know what I think about myself," I said, touching my cheek.

"Oh, you mean your face and the scar? That's nothing. You're a beautiful girl. But I guess you could have enemies."

"I suppose we all do."

"No. Don't be a romantic. Some people never have enemies. They don't have lovers, either. But I think you have. I should look around, if I were you." She finished her coffee, and stood up to go. "Tim's not going to the police. Doesn't want any fuss about the arsenic."

"No, Tim's not brave." She walked towards the door.

"He's brave," I said. "He's a realist."

"I'll let myself out."

I finished the coffee myself and enjoyed it. I thought Lynn Alloway was outrageous and knew it and counted on it.

But, as far as outrageousness went, I thought I had the edge on her.

The next day I worked very hard at my dictionary of recipes. In addition I did some research into a new way of cooking gâteau génoise. In spite of this I didn't sleep but lay in my bed wide-eyed for hours. The next night was the same. But the third day I felt relaxed and cheerful. In spite of my forebodings it seemed that nothing was going to happen after all. I had a lucky day. An unconventional recipe of coeur à la crème came out beautifully, and I baked a cherry savarin that was like a dream. I went to bed and slept well. Perhaps I shouldn't have done, but I was very tired.

While I was asleep a stranger came into town. In the

morning, he called on me. He told me he was a detective. And for the first time I learned that I, Anna Barclay, was suspected of having poisoned fifteen people.

3

He was a young man, quietly and unobtrusively dressed.
I suppose detectives have to be. I liked him. That was
the strange thing. I liked him and trusted him at once.
I'd never thought of charm as a quality that detectives
have to have. But when you think about it, you can see
how practical such an asset can be. And he liked me, too.
I suppose he in his turn never expected a poisoner to have
charm, although everything goes to show that George
Joseph Smith and Dr. Pritchard and Madeleine Smith
must have had it in plenty. And people thought Seddon
trustworthy into the bargain. You see, I know a lot about
poisoners now. I've been reading it up.

I was suspected of having poisoned fifteen people,
twelve of them children.

It seemed an extraordinary, simple, even common-
place approach to come and ask me, the suspect, about it.
But he was incredibly gentle and kind in his questions.
He made you want to tell.

I had finished breakfast and was studying an old
cookery book, dated 1825 and printed in Boston, when
Mrs. Twining showed in my visitor. I was to get to know
him so well, so well, but then he was new to me.

She opened her mouth to introduce him, but he got
there first. "Miss Barclay?" he said rapidly. "James Dilke."

"I don't know you."

"No." He sounded regretful. "No, I'm afraid you don't. But I have various papers here with my name on. You can read them."

He handed me a small folder. "No." I shook my head.

"Please do. I want you to." He handed me the papers again. I looked, not really seeing: his photograph, an identification card, a letter with formal official heading. He took them back and shook his head slightly. "You really ought to read things that are put before you. But in this case, as it happens, you're all right."

"What you mean is that *you* are all right?" I was beginning to get angry.

"Yes, that's right." He smiled. "Can we talk here? Will we be undisturbed?"

"I can't promise anything," I said.

"It really would be preferable if we are undisturbed." He was calm, unhurried.

"Who *are* you?"

"You didn't read what I gave you . . . I'm a detective."

Mrs. Twining came in with a tray, on which were a coffee pot and two cups. She was pink with curiosity, so I knew she had been listening at the door. There was no need for her to act the well-trained servant, it wasn't what she was paid for at all. I didn't want any coffee; neither, I suspect, did James Dilke. But he politely accepted a cup and put it on the table by him. At no time in his visit did he attempt to drink any of it.

Of course, I was thinking of the past. This was why I was nervous. People who have suppressed the truth in the past can never face the police as openly as those who have hidden nothing. But nothing stays hidden forever. When the surface of the land is disturbed, whether to build a palace or a farmhouse, or even to dig a ditch, no matter that these one day fall into disuse and dereliction, to lie beneath the soil again, the scar across the fields always remains to the discerning eye. It's strange it should be so. I could hardly believe it when an archaeologist told me, but now I know it must be true of all wounds. They are marked there indelibly in the marrow; you carry the scar for good.

I looked at him nervously. He saw this: he was trained to see such things. Perhaps he even became a detective because he had a naturally perceptive eye.

"You live all by yourself, do you, Miss Barclay?"

"Yes."

"It must be lonely for you."

"Is that what you came to ask me?"

"No . . . I'm trying to help you, Miss Barclay. You seem to me a little tense."

"I didn't think detectives did help people. That's not usually their purpose, is it?"

"As it happens, it is part of mine," he said quietly. "I want to ask you some questions and I want you to answer me with freedom and without constraint. You won't do that if I have alarmed you."

From the kitchen I could hear music coming from the transistor Mrs. Twining always carried in her pocket and used when my record player was, as now, not available to her. She had captured an orchestra playing Richard Strauss. *Till Eulenspiegel* it was, but the playing lacked punch. The kitchen door closed, cutting off the sound just before Till is hanged. I wasn't sorry to miss this strident moment.

"Miss Barclay, I believe you hire yourself out as a cook?" I saw his gaze move round my sitting-room with its Toile do Jouy walls, its Lowry painting and its David Wynne bronze. "In fact, you are a professional cook?"

"Yes." I didn't help him off the hook, although there is as much difference between my cooking and that of the average cook as there is between haute couture and the little dressmaker round the corner. "Among other things."

"Yes. I was coming to the other things. You make sweets and give them to your friends. A sort of fudge?"

"It's not fudge." I closed my eyes briefly. My delicious and expensive sweetmeat is not fudge, in the name of which many horrors are perpetrated.

"Do you read the newspapers, Miss Barclay?"

"I see one every day. I don't read every word."

"Do you read the local newspaper?"

I shook my head.

"Do you lead a rather withdrawn life, Miss Barclay?"

46

"I wouldn't call it that."

"A lot of people would." He sounded abstracted, as if he wasn't really thinking about this part of our exchange. "In fact, dangerously so. Hasn't it ever struck you that it *could* be dangerous?"

"Isolation and ignorance must always be dangerous," I said slowly.

"But you don't think you are in that state?"

"I must be, in some way, if you are here," I said, even more slowly.

"Good. We've got somewhere. You are loosening up, Miss Barclay." Then he said, "So you haven't heard about the children?"

"What children?"

He looked at me strangely. "Oh come, Miss Barclay. There are no children that come into your mind as being associated with you?"

"I know one child." But Peter was growing up now. I'd said so myself. No longer was he a child.

"You don't necessarily have to know these children," he said, a trifle grimly.

I stared. My heart-beat, which had already quickened, became noisier, and I could feel the pulse in my throat. "A group of children?" I said through dry lips, a picture forming in my mind of children round a school door.

"Yes, the children at the Lamb's Hill Remedial Centre Day School. It's a school for children with physical disabilities of various sorts. Some are lame. Some spastic. Some have had bad acidents. All are physically frail."

"They were at the school gate, waiting for the school bus," I said. "It was raining. One of them was crying. He didn't really have any legs. No legs at all. I wanted to cheer him up. I had some bags of montelimar and marchpane I was taking, I was taking . . ." I faltered. Where had I been taking it? "I gave some to the children."

"Silly girl," he said, in a level, almost expressionless tone.

"I wanted to help."

"And now you know what trouble it can bring."

"What happened to them?"

"Let me tell you a story," he said carefully. "It seems

47

the children ate the sweets that were given to them. They all fell ill. Two sisters were particularly ill. They recovered. But one child is desperately ill and will probably die. That's the story."

I heard myself draw in a breath and expel it sharply. I felt quite outside myself. It could have been another person doing it.

"Which child?" I heard myself say. "The boy?"

He looked at me hard. "You do know about the boy, then?"

"My sweets couldn't kill him," I said.

"No? All the sweets were eaten, so perhaps we will never know for sure. But, supposing traces of arsenic were . . ." he hesitated, then said, "detected in the sweet bags . . ."

"It *can't* be anything to do with me."

"No? I think it *was* something to do with you, all the same. But let's leave that. Go on to something else, but related. I'll come straight out and tell you," he said. "You understand when you are looking for the cause of sickness among a group of people that various tests are run on excreta and waste as a matter of routine? The doctors are looking primarily for bacterial or viral strains." He paused, he was an unconscious actor, waiting to get his effect. "They *did* turn up traces of bacterial strains that hang about the human race. We're the dirtiest of animals, you know." He raised his eyebrows as if he, personally, cleaned out his bacteria every day. "But all the strains they detected were what they call benign. In other words, we can live with them and get along. So they didn't cause any trouble." Once again he paused. "No, what other tests turned up in minute traces was arsenic."

"Traces of arsenic turn up naturally," I heard myself say.

"You seem to know something about arsenic, Miss Barclay," he said quietly.

"I've read about it."

"Well, you're right, of course, traces of arsenic do turn up under completely natural and innocent conditions."

I didn't like the way he said innocent.

"I haven't poisoned anyone," I said, and my voice seemed loud in my ears.

"I understand people have been asking questions." Again that careful way of putting it. "I'm surprised you haven't heard. One or two of us are trying to find an answer."

"I don't believe they can have come to harm through any action of mine."

He looked at me; I felt him studying my face. He was trying to assess me, as I was trying to assess him. He took his coat from the chair, preparing to go.

"This cooking you do—have you asked yourself why you do it?" he said, in a different tone of voice from any he had used till now.

I didn't answer.

"You may think you have the answer. But ask yourself what it does for you, what it does for the people who employ you? Don't you see the position you have put yourself into?"

I stared.

"Ask yourself what it all adds up to."

No words of reply came into my mouth. I didn't know what to say.

"Goodbye," he said, with surprising gentleness, and was gone.

After he had left, I went upstairs to my bedroom, opened all my drawers one by one, and searched them. Then I turned my search to the long wall cupboard where I kept my clothes. I shook my dresses and felt in the pockets of every coat. I turned up my shoes, I even took a chair and searched the high shelf where I kept hats and handbags. Nowhere did I make a discovery of anything hidden.

Then I went downstairs and repeated the search in my sitting-room, where I opened every drawer in my desk. I did the same thing, slowly and methodically, in my kitchen.

When I had finished I felt sure that there was no poison to be found in my house.

"Nice man," said Mrs. Twining, bustling into the room

again. "I didn't take to him at first, but towards the end I quite liked him."

"He'll bear watching," I said, controlling my voice.

"You're trembling all over," cried Mrs. Twining.

And it was only when she said this that I understood I had been terrified of him.

4

The nightmare began then. From the day of his call on me nothing settled down again into its right place. It was as if I had been into a new country, seen things arranged as they were not at home, and could never, ever again relax into my old ways of looking at my own world. Continually now it disposed itself into carefully composed, strange vistas, like a newly discovered landscape. Once before I had had this happen to me with the physical world, after a visit to Venice, when the very woods and houses of home appeared to shape themselves before my eyes into a Giorgione or a Bellini landscape. But this time it went beyond the physical and into the mental world.

I tried to master it, and for a moment I really thought I had. I tidied up Jackson's cage, and shut him firmly in (he looked at me sadly; he was a sad bird in those days). I cleaned through the house. Mrs. Twining had already done it today and would do it tomorrow, but no matter, I did it again. I started to sort through my B recipes for my dictionary (baba à rhum, bouillebaisse) but I couldn't settle. So I went for a walk.

I tried not to go near St. John's, but I could not keep away. There it lay before me, a beautiful object, as always.

It represented lots of things I loved, but sometimes, I thought, things I hated too.

I concentrated on the things I loved. St. John's embodied harmony, grace and what the classical age knew as the "golden mean." But I knew its beauty rested on certain assumptions about the world that I couldn't quite stomach, like privilege, and that it demanded a good deal of people's time and life and energy to keep it beautiful. And finally I knew that it was a lie and a fraud and a deception, because half of it was phony, it had a scar down the middle.

I put my hand to my face, all my bad thoughts back in full bloom.

Slowly I walked down through the trees, heavy oak and chestnut. Nearer to the road was a belt of lime trees and I stood there, enjoying their sweet scent. Then I walked on again down the hill. The geography of this piece of land is such that from half way down the hill you can see across the peninsula on which we all live and on which our houses are scattered, you can see the main road stretching from the coast inland to the city. It is far enough away for us to feel inviolate, but it is within sight. As I stood there, I saw a battered old Land-Rover, painted dark yellow, which I recognised as belonging to my farmer-suitor. Well, there's somebody who loves me, I thought. Or my cooking. Looking at the uneasy progress of his car, I thought what he needed in a wife was an engineering knowledge too. I remembered he had taken me to a motor rally or two. (All farmers love rushing around in old cars, pretending to be tough. It used to be horses, now it's the old banger. I suppose it soothes the feeling in them that they aren't really competing.) I waved to him. He couldn't see me, but I waved anyway.

I hurried on down the hill. If I walked fast across the curving belt of trees, if I hurried, I could cross our side road and get to where the main road came close to us in time to meet his car. I thought suddenly I'd like to speak to him as to a cheerful voice from outside. Often he maddened me, but now I thought he was cheerful and safe. He would put his arm round my shoulders and say hello, Anna, old girl, and really be pleased to see me. Perhaps he didn't miss me much when I wasn't there, probably his feelings didn't go very deep, but he liked me when he saw me, in a simple uncomplicated kind of way. I wouldn't marry him, of course. Couldn't indeed. But just now I thought I wasn't above taking a little of the amusement he could offer. Not very kind of me, but I wasn't feeling kind.

The car was coming down the main road all right, my sense of timing was impeccable. I approached slowly, knowing he could see me. Then I waited. I thought, he'll see me, stop the car, and come bouncing out.

I halted. I was almost ready to wave. I *did* wave. He didn't stop. The car did not slacken its speed. In a moment, I thought he hadn't seen me. Then I knew he had. He gave a stiff, embarrassed bow and drove on.

I stood there for a moment, staring. The episode was like a little trickle of cold water down my skin. I shivered. The day was hot, but I knew what it was to feel cold.

I was in a fury of emotions. I was angry. I was frightened. I was enjoying myself. I was lost. For a moment I hardly saw the placid English landscape. Suddenly I was walking across a landscape which was full of pointed rocks, strange traps and pools ringed with flowers in which strange monsters lurked. It was terrifying to be me, and yet immensely exciting.

I didn't accuse John Fisher, my former suitor, of malice, but he was a deeply conventional man and something of a gossip. He had heard gossiping tales about me and had been frightened off. I knew one thing then; he didn't love me.

I turned back, inwards towards the sheltered pasture in which lay our houses and St. John's. I knew I had to go back. Inwards lay the answer to so many of the questions that now perplexed me. Whether I was wise or even safe to go back was another issue. How strange it is to be completely at home in a place and yet at risk. But it was so for me then.

I went home, let Jackson out of his cage (from which he sped with a happy squawk) and sat at my desk, working on my recipes. That is to say, I sat there turning them over, without really thinking about them. The telephone on my desk rang. I ignored it for a little while, then lifted it. There was silence for a moment, then a voice asked huskily:

"Did you know you are being watched?"

"Who's that speaking?" I said sharply.

"Did you know you are being watched?"

I didn't know the voice. It wasn't an educated one, nor particularly friendly. Not unfriendly, either. It sounded neutral.

"Who are you?"

"Did you know you are being watched?"

"Say something else," I cried.

"Nothing else," it said.

I slammed the receiver down. I hated calls like this. We had had a plague of them lately, not usually much to the point. This one might be. I was beginning to see what my visitor had meant when he asked me did I know what position I was being placed in. I was being placed in the dock, and a verdict of guilty was being prepared. I didn't think it was accident or chance. Everything that was happening to me had the horrible feeling of being meant.

Then I thought I would make a telephone call on my own account. I dialled. Lynn Alloway answered.

"How's Tim?" I asked.

"Better." She was terse. I wasn't her favourite woman. I wasn't anybody's favourite. Then it appeared her bad humour was not directed at me. "And he's in a bloody foul mood," she said. "Where have you been all day?"

"In and out."

"I've been trying to contact you for hours."

"Oh?"

"Yes, I'm thinking of giving another dinner party soon. I wanted to book you."

I was surprised. Apparently I wasn't as unpopular as I'd thought. "When will this be?"

"I haven't quite worked on that yet. Soon. Next week, maybe."

"Large party?"

"No. No, I don't think so." She seemed vague.

I drew my engagement pad towards me. "We'll have to meet and discuss the food you want."

"Oh, like before," she said.

54

"What, exactly the same?" She could certainly surprise me. Was she planning to poison her husband again?

"Oh, yes. It was a success, wasn't it? I mean, in its way."

"I should have thought you'd like a change."

"You mean because of Tim? Oh, I'm not superstitious. Anyway, he's asked for it. It's what he wants, he says." There was a faint, faint hint of amusement in her voice. I thought she had got her husband hanging up on some hook and was watching him manoeuvre; not squirm, clever Tim Alloway would never do anything so ridiculous as squirm.

I put my engagement pad aside. "Let me know when you've settled on a day," I said. "And how many guests you plan."

"I think that'll be the same as before." She sounded thoughtful.

"It should be a good little party," I said, and put down the telephone.

With the unpredictability of life, she would probably hold it, and have a great success, and we would all be as happy as kings. Even me, in the kitchen.

Jackson was flapping his wings and making angry noises at the window. He seemed to have a lot of enemies and I thought he'd probably seen one. I walked to the window.

Ben Drummond was just getting out of his car. He saw me, and raised his hand in what I thought, erroneously, was a greeting. What he was really saying was: I'm coming in and don't try and keep me out.

"You here on your own?" he said, as soon as he was inside the door.

"Yes, of course."

"Mrs. Twining?"

"She goes home at twelve. Why? What is this?"

"Never mind what we've pretended or haven't pretended. What we haven't said to each other. What I've closed my eyes to."

I stood up. "Ben!"

"The child is dead."

"What are you saying to me?" I whispered. I wanted to make my voice loud and angry, but I couldn't do it, it *would* come out frightened.

"The child is dead."

"What child?"

"I can't bear it when you talk like that, Anna," he said his voice jerky.

I stared at him speechlessly.

"I like you to be always honest with me, Anna. You have been in the past, I know that. Only, no longer. You don't tell me everything. I've been conscious of that. Don't pretend. You know which child."

Jackson flew forward with a screech, and fluttered to the top of the bookcase by the door, where he perched. eyeing us, and moving his wings restlessly.

"I've kept quiet about all the talk that's been growing around you. I know you never bother to read the newspapers. You're isolated here in this little island where we live. You like being isolated. But outside there's a world that doesn't like you very much . . . those children. What did you *do* to them, Anna?"

Not all scenes have a logical ending. Logically, I suppose I should have thrown a fit of emotion. Screamed at him, or wept. One way or another I should have reacted. Instead I stood there, frozen, cold, quite unable to say a word. A window on a new world had opened to me. All the time I had been going about my life, cooking, choosing clothes, getting my hair washed, this wall of suspicion had been building up all round me. Without my knowing it, people had been considering me, weighing me up and finally concluding I could be a poisoner. A poisoner of a particularly nasty sort, moreover. There was a woman called Madeleine Pollock, she lived in a small Worcestershire town in the second half of the nineteenth century. Her father had been an apothecary in a small way of business. When he died, his shop was closed, and I suppose she had a fair amount of his stock left on her hands. At all events, she took to using up his supply of arsenic by mixing it with sweetmeats and candies and handing out pokes of it to the local children. I'd always imagined that she gave them striped bullseyes, smelling of peppermint, and transparent acid-drops and golden sugar barley. Madeleine Pollock was cunning about the way she handed out her poisoned presents, and several children died before she was caught. She was only a frail little Victorian lady, but she left her mark on social history. My father hadn't been an apothecary with a shop full of drugs to leave behind to me, but apparently I was suspected of being this type of poisoner. They had a special theory about Miss Pollock back in nineteenth-century Worcestershire; she was a "poisoner for pleasure." They had a special name for her; she was Poisoning Polly. I too was a Poisoning Polly.

"I've had the police here," I said.

"What, already? I didn't know it had gone that far." He seemed taken aback.

"Well, one policeman anyway."

"What did he say to you, Anna?"

I shrugged. I wasn't going into all that with Ben. He could think about it for himself. He would do, as well. I could see him starting on the process.

"Anny, what sort of a person was he?" he began.

"Ordinary."

"Senior? Or someone unimportant just doing a routine call?"

"Oh, senior," I said, remembering the man. "There was nothing routine about his visit."

"Things must have gone a long way, then. I don't like it, Anny. It's gone further than I thought."

I didn't answer.

"Don't you see, Anny? It means they must have suspected you from the beginning."

"I begin to see that you did," I said.

"Don't let's quarrel, Anny."

"We seem to be started on it," I said. "A little disagreement is starting up without any help from either of us."

"Don't be bitter."

"Perhaps you would like me to say thank you for thinking me a poisoner."

"Come and sit down, Anna, and let's talk this over."

He drew me to the sofa and made me sit down. From where we sat I could see through the open window. I sat there and watched the trees moving in the wind. "We have to decide what to do."

"Who was the child who died? What was his name and where did he live?"

"Why do you want to know?"

"I want to give a name, a face to him. Surely you can understand this?"

"Understand, yes. Not like it. I feel as though the less you know the better."

"You mean you don't want me to think about it," I said. "But all the same, you are forcing me to do so." It was so like Ben; he was always ambivalent in his attitude to me. He always wanted to protect me and yet to show me life at the same time. Perhaps all men are the same and often you get a kiss and a knife to cut yourself together.

"He was called Philip Cowan; he was eleven. If you want to know what he looked like he was small for his age and dark. That enough?"

"Yes. Thank you." We were engaged in open hostility now.

"I'm asking you to be careful, Anny," he said. "Talk is starting up about Tim Alloway getting a dose of arsenic."

I stared at him and he flushed.

"*I* haven't said anything," he said. "And naturally, I wouldn't encourage anyone to say anything to me."

"So this is just hearsay?"

"Anna!" He controlled himself, and went on in a consciously quiet and controlled tone: "I don't think you've grasped what the feeling has been like in the neighbourhood."

"I haven't noticed anything." But had Mrs. Twining been trying to tell me? She'd made several odd remarks. She was always protective of me.

"No." His voice was crisp. "You wouldn't, isolated here in this spot. Oh it's lovely, I like it, but it's out of the real world. But the real world can break in, Anna."

As always when faced with a challenge of this sort, I touched my cheek, an action which I knew frightened Ben. He had learnt not to say anything, but I saw his lips tighten.

"Well, I suppose you'd better marry me," he said.

"Thank you. That's a really appealing invitation."

"So that I can protect you," he said furiously.

"*What* a happy marriage we should have."

"*Please,* Anna."

"Anyway, it's out of the question."

"Well, if you won't marry me, at least stay at home," he said gloomily.

"I won't even promise that."

"Don't *talk* to anyone then." He looked at me. "It's all right, you needn't promise. It's what you're good at, anyway, not saying much."

"It's what I'm good at," I agreed. My hand dropped away from my cheek.

We stood looking at each other in silence. Then I spoke, phrasing my words deliberately: "I swear I did nothing that could have harmed the child. Any child. I don't have any poison. Any poison."

"I hope you don't have any, Anna." He added hurriedly, "I mean I hope nothing has crept into your kitchen supplies by mistake."

"Not my mistake."

"There *is* Tim Alloway," he said wretchedly.

"Bother Tim Alloway," I said.

He moved away. "I think I'd better go, Anna."

"Yes, I think you had."

"Stay inside, that's all."

"I haven't got any arsenic," I called after him angrily, in a loud voice. I heard him bang his car door. He was angry too.

As soon as he had gone I tried to find the bit of paper on which I had written the name of the dead child, but I couldn't find it. Ben must have taken it with him. Another device to protect me, no doubt. His name might represent dangerous knowledge for me. Probably he already regretted having told me the name.

I wasn't as brave as I had made Ben think. Inside I felt quite frightened. Angry, but apprehensive. I knew people were talking about me, accusing me. I was prepared for a rough time. But I didn't, yet, feel physically afraid. I didn't think I was in any danger. I couldn't imagine any situation like that hitting me.

I suppose I just don't have an inventive mind.

When I heard Ben's car depart, I knew it was time to capture Jackson and put him back in his cage. He was a dreadful old bird in many ways, fierce and unrepentant, yet strangely congenial to me. I had had ambivalent feelings for him ever since he had turned up on my doorstep, neatly caged, one autumn morning, an unlikely foundling. Mrs. Twining had a theory that he had been left at my house by mistake and ought really to have been delivered elsewhere. Perhaps. But at all events he made himself at home and joined in my life intemperately as often as he could. He was particularly fond of savaging the small objects on my dressing table, lifting up bottles and knocking them, carrying off small objects in his beak and chewing them. He seemed to hate my lipsticks. And certain smells, such as that of my bath oil, obviously irritated him. Now I wanted him out of my way for the moment.

We scowled at each other from opposite sides of his cage, but I had the last word because I could always cover his cage with a cloth, and against this he had no redress. I stood by his cage for a moment, listening, but he was quiet.

I went into my bedroom and cleaned my face, then put on a bathrobe. Next I went into my bathroom and turned on the hot tap. When the water was running, I poured in plenty of my favourite bath oil. As the rich geranium smell floated out, I could hear a rustle from behind Jackson's shroud. He knew what I was doing, and was probably gnashing his teeth. He was an old puritan, really.

My bath oil, which was called "Mousseline," and was only used by me as part of a special ritual, smelt feminine, rich and delicious. When I used it I felt feminine, rich and delicious too. That was all my ritual amounted to. It was a cure of that mood which was not depression but close to it, compounded of sadness, loneliness and anxiety. A thin, whining mood, the opposite of self-love. My ritual restored my self-esteem. I was a better person when I stepped out of the bath, or at any rate, easier to live with, than when I got into it. I had no faith that the magic would work now against the welter of emotions that beset me, but I knew it would help.

The sweet waters lapped about me, not comforting me as much as usual, but helping. I was calmer when I emerged. No longer so angry with Ben, I could almost see his point of view.

After what seemed a long quiet time, I got out of the bath and went to the telephone.

I hoped that Tim Alloway was still too unwell to come to the telephone, because it was his wife I wished to talk to. Lynn answered the telephone. She sounded surprised it was me.

"Oh, hello."

"I want to ask you something."

"Yes?" She was cautious, no promises.

"Why did you ask me to come and cook another meal for you again?"

"Well, I've said, it was a success . . ."

"Was it because you wanted to help me? Because you'd heard talk about me, accusing me of being a poisoner?"

"I haven't heard anything."

"But you didn't think of issuing the invitation on your own, did you? Someone asked you to do it, didn't they?"

"You ask a lot of questions," she said dryly.

"Let me guess who it was without asking again. I guess it was Ben."

"I love that scent you use."

"What's that got to do with it."

"More than you might think." She gave that rich laugh of hers. "Tells me the sort of person you are."

I was silent. "Mousseline" did indeed tell you quite a lot about me, but you couldn't smell it over the telephone wires. She seemed to have a special sensitivity towards me, this woman.

"And about the people you like."

She still had me guessing. "Mind you," she went on. "I think there's a side to you that particular scent doesn't reflect. I mean, you're quite an aggressive little character, aren't you?"

There didn't seem to be any particular answer to that one. I thought she was just throwing up a smoke screen to make me drop the subject I had started on. "You don't want me to ask again about Ben, so I won't. But you've already answered me."

I put the receiver down. It seemed to me that her laugh sounded as I did so.

I wasn't laughing. Lynn Alloway had fended off my questions nicely, but in doing so, of course, she had given herself away. She *was* hiding something.

For a little while I read, and then I slept. Without effort I slid into deep, quiet sleep. If I dreamt, the dreams were so swift and light that I was unconscious of them.

In the depths of my sleep not only was I blind but I was also deaf. No sound got through. Perhaps there was very little to hear.

Ben had often said I should get a dog. Dogs hear things, he said, dogs bark at strange noises, dogs can alert you. He knew what he was talking about.

Perhaps I did hear something without realising it and this was why I stirred. Or perhaps one sense is always on the watch. I shall never know why, in the small hours, I woke.

I woke and lay there for a moment in the dark. Then I sneezed. I knew now why I was awake.

I could smell smoke.

Some smoke smells are delicious, redolent of wood and leaves, one of the minor pleasures of life. But other smoke, thin and acrid, rings alarm in the mind at once. This smoke did so to me now, it wasn't an *innocent* smell.

I sat up, pulled on my dressing gown, and put on the lamp by my bed. The room was tranquil and undisturbed, the blue sprigged curtains moving slightly in the breeze from my open window, the matching bed cover neatly folded over the chair. The room had been tidy when I went to bed, it was tidy still, nothing had disturbed it. Yet I smelt smoke . . .

I'm frightened of fire. Not everybody knows this about me, but people close to me, like Ben and Mrs. Twining, know that even to light a match costs me a pang. Now I could feel my throat tightening and my heart beating fast.

I opened my bedroom door and an evil frond of thick grey smoke curled up from the stair-well by my feet.

My house is small, the staircase narrow and curving,

but I knew I had to go down it into that pit of smoke.

I could scream, but no one would hear. No one would ever hear anything. I'm such a coward, about fire anyway, that I was prepared almost to stand there silently staring. Then I heard Jackson cough down below. I suppose parrots can cough? Whatever the noise he achieved, it was strangely human and moving. I knew I couldn't let the bird choke to death and I had to save him.

I forced myself to put first one foot then the other on the stairs. Even so, I stood for a long moment feeling sick. But the smell of smoke grew stronger. Fear often forces the coward to choose between two fears. A choice of this sort can, paradoxically, make the coward braver. I feared the fire, but I feared even more to leave Jackson to die.

I pushed on down the stairs, hanging on to the banister, not for support, but as a lever. Every time my hand left the rail it went back to push me forward. As I descended, my intelligence began sorting out the elements in the smoke. First there was a sweetish smell that I thought was paper burning, but then there came a gust of throat-catching, stinking black smoke that meant something much worse. Paper is vegetable burning, this was a man-made smell. My guess was plastic, smouldering stickily.

So then I knew that the fire was in my kitchen. And if I had been frightened before, I was now terrified. Because beyond the kitchen was the oil tank on which all the heating of the house depended. The tank had been filled only three days ago.

Jackson and I not only had enough oil to burn us, we had enough to blow us to the moon first.

Then the lights on the stairs went out.

Cowards like me take precautions against their fears. I had had a fire extinguisher fixed on the wall by the kitchen. I moved down the stairs and slid my hand towards the ledge where the fire extinguisher rested.

My fingers reached into emptiness, crawled over the shelf. Nothing. I took a second to understand that the extinguisher was truly gone. But with realisation came the conviction that it had not gone by accident. Someone had removed it.

I was coughing myself by this time. The smoke was

63

thick down here near the kitchen door. I hesitated about opening it, because I had heard that with a fire you should keep the doors closed to hinder its spreading. I didn't want to open the door. I knew I had to, though, because Jackson was in the kitchen. He coughed again and then I thought: No, he isn't. I left him in the sitting-room last night.

This door, to my left, was slightly ajar, just as I had left it. I stumbled through, getting used to the dark and seized Jackson's cage. He was alive, all right. He thumped around reassuringly in his cage.

I had now to get myself and Jackson out of the house. The window seemed nearest, but I couldn't get it open. I was making heavy weather of all this, and I knew it. Jackson gave a heavy jump in his cage.

"Oh, shut up," I said, but somehow he had helped. I turned from the window and stumbled back through the room in the direction of the front door. A wave of heat thrust at me from the direction of the kitchen.

The front door was locked and bolted. I set Jackson's cage on the ground and fumbled. The lock turned easily enough, the bolt moved back, but the door did not budge.

"I'm frightened, Jackson," I said. But he knew it; he was already squawking away from the bottom of his cage.

I remember saying aloud: I can't get out, I can't get out. I was shaking at the door in my panic, hardly taking in what was happening. Then I steadied a little and through mindless fear came a little hard fact of perception. The door was sticking at one point.

I ran my hand slowly along the bottom edge of the door. It was wedged with a piece of wood. I clawed at it with my nails of my second finger and thumb. The wedge came away.

I opened the door and fell into the garden, carrying the bird in the cage with me. I sat on the step outside the house and breathed deeply. My heart was still thumping, and I felt sick. Jackson called out to me and I straightened his cage. The covering had fallen off in our struggles and I could see his eyes glittering. The moon came from behind a cloud and lit up the landscape. I stood up and turned to stare at my house.

Fire always awakens deep, irrational fears inside me. Even now, outside and safe, I felt sick and weak. I could see flames licking at the windows and smell the pungent smoke of burning wood, paint and plastic. I stared, wondering what to do next, when I heard movement behind me.

5

I was terrified. For one moment I was too frightened even to turn around, and then I heard Jackson enunciate clearly, "Ha, ha, ha, ha!" It didn't mean he was having a joke, it just meant he'd seen someone he knew.

I swung round. "Ben!" I said. "What are you doing here?"

"I might ask you that." He hurried up the path towards me. "I was out on a late call and saw you at the door." Behind him I could just see his car parked on the road. "I was alarmed. I didn't know it was you at first, and thought you were having a caller. I thought I ought to come and investigate." He looked alarmed. "I'd better get some help. How did it start?"

"I *have* had a visitor," I said slowly.

He was taking in my appearance. "Anny, you're hurt."

"No. No, just frightened."

"Your hand. There's blood all over it."

I raised it and looked. What he said was quite true. There was blood on my right hand. "It's my nail," I said. "I've got a splinter under it."

But he was already examining it. I winced as his fingers probed mine. "I'll pull that out if you can stand it . . . I'll get my bag."

"We ought to see to the fire first," I said weakly. While

66

we were talking the fire could be spreading. I could smell the smoke.

"I'll do this first. You're in pain. Hang on, Anna." His voice was fading from my ears and a cold darkness settling on my eyes. Distantly, I heard him saying, "Darling . . ."

When I came round I was on the grass, wrapped in what seemed to be his coat. Jackson, out of his cage, was looking at me lugubriously from the grass. I struggled to sit up.

"Lie down again, Anny." Ben walked back towards me. "Give yourself a minute more. You went right out. But I did your finger." I glanced down at my finger, now wearing a neat bit of plaster.

"Thanks."

"I've had a look at your kitchen." He sat down beside me on the grass. "The fire is out now."

"How?"

"It hadn't got all that much of a hold. You lost your head. It's a mess in there, though."

"I believe you," I said with feeling.

"But it could have been nasty, Anny. In a little while it would have got a fine grip. How did it happen?"

"I have no idea." I did have some ideas, but I didn't want to think about them. "Accidents happen."

"Yes, sure." He was frowning. "You don't remember doing anything, throwing a match in that big box of paper? It was that that was alight first, I'd say, and then the big plastic waste bin started next."

"No match," I said.

"Sometimes you do these things automatically," he said.

I shook my head. "I'd have known if I'd struck a match. I'm frightened of them."

"What about that fire extinguisher you have?" he said, standing up himself, and helping me to my feet. "Why didn't you use it?"

"It wasn't there. It had gone."

He gave me a long look. "It was still there, Anny," he said. "I've just used it."

"*Not* on the shelf?" I said.

"Well, just underneath. It must have fallen."

"Or someone moved it," I said.

We looked at each other. "The door was wedged," I said.

"Wedged?"

"A thin piece of wood was stuck under the door. I moved it. I had to."

"So *that's* how you hurt your hand?"

"Yes."

"And you think someone put it there to jam the door."

"Yes."

He hummed a little tune. His eyes had a puzzled expression. There was something he didn't want to say.

"From the *inside,* Anny?"

It seems extraordinary that I had not seen the significance of this before. The person who had wedged the door had been on the inside. For that matter, so had the person who started the fire and moved the extinguisher.

If there was such a person. I could read Ben's doubts in his face. He didn't want me to see he had these doubts, but he was troubled. He loved me, he had often told me so, and I believed it to be true. But all the same he was wondering if I had created this fire myself.

"I'm not an arsonist," I said. "If that's what you're thinking."

"No, Anny, no." He flushed. He would be a jealous husband if I ever did marry him; there was something in him that watched me. "Anny, it's a good thing you woke up and got out."

"I'm terrified of fire."

"I know."

"I owe it to Jackson," I said, looking down at that morose bird.

"Perhaps it's a good thing you've got him after all." It was about the first friendly thing he had ever said about Jackson.

"I sometimes thought that *you* gave him to me."

Ben laughed. "Never."

We went back into the house. I was quite steady now. The place felt smoky, and a look in the kitchen had convinced me that no more cooking would be done in there for some time.

"It's a bit worse in there than you gave me to understand," I said in a restrained way to Ben.

"I didn't want to alarm you."

"I'm not alarmed now."

"No, I must say you seem calm enough."

I wasn't so calm inside as I appeared, but I was calm enough to think about my appearance. The dawn had come up and a pale light was over everything. In the mirror I could see I had black streaks on my face and my hair was dishevelled. I had blood on my sleeve and I had torn a hole in my gown.

"Let's have a talk," Ben said.

"I must tidy up." My voice was unsteady.

He looked at me professionally, "Yes, you do that. And I'll make some coffee—if the kitchen'll rise to it."

I combed my hair, and washed my hands and face. The blood came away easily. I was beginning to have that empty drained feeling you get after a period of physical strain. It's not true about things looking better in the morning. Some things look infinitely worse.

Ben appeared at my bedroom door. "No coffee. The power's off."

"Oh yes." I remembered. "I should have told you."

"I've got some brandy, though." He produced a bottle from behind his back.

"That's what I use for cooking," I said.

"Knowing the way you cook, I expect it's drinkable."

It was, in fact, a good brandy. You can't cook well with poor materials. But I didn't want it. "No brandy," I said.

"Yes. You need something. I can give you a shot of something from my bag, if you prefer, but a stimulant of some sort you need now." He poured a modest drink for us both. "We need to have a talk and this is as good a time as ever. It's brought things to a head."

"I don't want to talk."

"You've been avoiding me."

"No."

"Yes. And for some time, too."

"Not on purpose."

"Yes." Ben could be hard when he liked; he was hard now. "Deliberately, I'd say. Why?"

I was silent.

"You're keeping something from me. What is it?"

My hand wandered up to my cheek.

"Take your hand away," said Ben. "Do you know, whenever I get on to anything sensitive, you touch your cheek. Don't do it."

My hand dropped away.

"I know why you do it. Do you think I don't know that I did it to you? Do you think I ever, ever forget?"

I had thought he was too sophisticated, too full of self-knowledge, to blame himself for what was, really, an accident.

A fall from a tree at the age of eleven, a branch tearing into my face, an infection following, how could he really blame himself?

"*I* washed your cheek in that bloody stream," he said. "I ought to have known it had face rot in it." He used the slang viciously, as if by so doing he was exorcising the very ordinary bacteria, the *fusiformis,* which had invaded my wound.

"It wasn't your fault, my dear," I said.

Very rightly, he hated me for my softness. "It's what spoils everything between us," he said bitterly and gloomily.

"Do you think so?" I said.

"Doesn't it, doesn't it?" He took a step towards me, hope dawning. "Do you mean . . . Anna?"

I side-stepped. "Mind the brandy." I didn't want a proposal at this hour of the morning. Anyway, he was in a funny mood. He might not have taken a refusal.

"Oh, don't be so bloody womanly," he said. "I hate you like that."

I smiled; I always knew, when he showed temper, that, whatever the issue between us, he had lost and I had won. He drank his brandy in a gulp.

"You going to report this to the police, Anna?"

"According to you there isn't anything to report. Just a little accident with a lighted match."

"Yes." He looked thoughtful. "Tatiana," he said. "You're in real trouble."

He never called me Tatiana. But that is my real name:

70

Tatiana Barclay. When I was in America they taught me to call myself Anna.

My mother, whom I had hardly know, was well born. Extremely well born.

Not that I nourish romances that I am the secret great-great-granddaughter of a Czar (although there are family jokes about my great-grandmother's *real* father), but I am *hoch geboren,* as my stuffy German grandaunts still like to put it. After my father died, I went to live for a short time one summer with my German-Russian-American relations, and they instructed me, oh, not by direct precept, but by the way they themselves lived and spoke, to call myself Anna or Anny and not the lavish and romantic Tatiana. I am named after the heroine of Pushkin's poem *Eugene Onegin,* and she was a lady who knew what it was to love and be rejected. She met a tragedy and surmounted it. I thought I could do the same.

I had not stayed long with my mother's relations, although I had come to respect them if not to love them. Soon old Mrs. Despenser summoned me back to St. John's. I had cried bitterly when taken away from her that summer and she had said severely, "Never mind, Anny, go and visit your grand relations as your father wishes." Then she gave me a smile, and said, "Back at St. John's by Christmas." She had me back before the leaves were off the trees in the autumn and although I went away again it was never for long.

"You haven't called me that for years," I said.

"Called you what?"

"Tatiana."

"I was quite unconscious of it." He had flushed. "I never even think of you as Tatiana. I suppose I was far back in the past. It doesn't even suit you. It's a wild name, full of pine forests and steppes and winter. You're not like that. You're gentle and calm. One of the gentlest people I know, Anny." His voice shook. "But you are in trouble. The sort of things that are happening to you don't happen by accident, Tim Alloway, the children, this fire. Can't you think of any reason for it? . . . isn't there anything you want to tell me?"

"Of course, I am keeping *some* things from you," I

said slowly. "It's always that way, isn't it? No communications between two people can be absolutely candid."

"I wish I could convince you that it needn't be that way with us."

"I can conceive of such a relationship," I said slowly. "With someone I loved passionately."

"I don't know what's come over you," he said. "You were perfectly normal till you went off for a holiday last winter. I don't feel I've known you ever since."

"Nothing happened while I was on holiday."

"And *that's* not true."

"I'm a normal enough person, but normal things don't happen to me," I said. "I feel like a prisoner in a fairy tale."

He stood up and put his brandy glass on the table. "Well, one thing's clear: you can't stay here."

"Why not?"

"The kitchen for one thing. And for another . . ." he hesitated.

"Yes."

"Well, perhaps there is feeling about you in this district about the child . . ." I made an involuntary cry of protest.

"Yes, of course, I know you are innocent," he said hastily. "That goes without saying, but you might be at risk. I think the fire was an accident . . . but I'm not quite sure."

I stared at him without speaking.

"It's that piece of wood," he said, speaking as if to himself. "Where did that come from?" For a moment he seemed far away, lost in some black place, then he came back to the room and addressed himself to me. "Get your things together. You'd better come and stay with me."

"With you? In that disorganised establishment you live in? No, thank you."

"Yes, I admit it's not too comfortable. And I daresay you'd better not come to me. Dolly Compton, then?"

I laughed. "No, *not* Dolly."

"No." Tacitly we both agreed that Dolly, bubbly, evanescent Dolly, was no hostess for a girl in trouble. She'd provide a spotlight rather than an umbrella.

"Lynn Alloway."

"No," I said, very firmly.

"There is one place you can go," he said slowly. "Servants to look after you, a well run house, position."

I waited, hardly breathing.

"It's not a house I like," he said, frowning. "But you would certainly be protected there. Welcomed, too."

"St. John's?" I said.

"Yes."

St. John's, beautiful old St. John's.

6

So there I was in St. John's where I had both feared and
longed to be. It was strange to be inside again. I had my
own room, where I had stayed before. I had simply met
Mrs. Franks in the hall and explained my disastrous fire,
and because she knew St. John's was a place where I
could come and go she simply carried my bags up for me,
while I carried Jackson in his cage. I put him on the table
by the window. It was hardly one of the grandest rooms
in the house, the sort of room you gave to a child or an
unimportant guest, but it had great charm. I put my
books and papers down on the old Davenport desk
against the wall. It was of walnut, bleached in the sun.
I think the charm of the room was that it had been
furnished about 1840 and never changed. It gave me
pleasure to see my things disposed about the room: my
little travelling clock on the marble shelf over the grate;
my leather framed photograph of my father. And, of
course, I had Jackson. It was ridiculous; I was in terrible
trouble, but I was madly happy.

Mrs. Franks came and stood in my room and watched
me unpack. "There's a woman come down from London
to cook for them," she announced. She always called her
employers "them," as if they belonged to a different
species. "They chose her in London themselves."

74

"Oh?" I was interested, professionally interested. "Good, do you think?"

"Scotch," said Mrs. Franks briefly. "Hands like spades on her. Don't know what she'd be like with the pastry. Makes a good cup of tea. Prefers Indian. I do myself. That's a good test of character, I say. Don't give me these China drinkers. You can't beat a good Himalayan tea. She prefers Ceylon herself, she says. Well, there's a lot to be said for Ceylon, needs to infuse a long while. All these good quality teas do."

"I know," I said.

"We've agreed to settle on a Darjeeling that she's going to order from Fortnums."

"Is she temporary?"

Mrs. Franks shrugged. "She seems to think she's here to stay, so it looks as if they're back for good, doesn't it? About time, too. Of course, they had their reasons for being away. The boy's improved, poor little fellow."

"You're fond of him, aren't you?"

"Always have been." She fidgeted with the curtain, pretending to straighten it, but really to hide her face. "I'm glad you're back, madam. You did right to come."

I stood very still, wondering if I had heard correctly, then I said softly, "Thank you."

She closed the door behind her, with her usual bang. She was an old gossip, and not famed for her hard work, but it was good to have a friend in the house. I wondered if I had any other.

There was a tap on the door. Polite, a little tentative. I knew who it was. I hoped he didn't mind that I was here.

"Hello, Peter," I said.

"I was out when you came," he said. "But I knew you were coming."

"Did you? I didn't know myself till a little while ago."

"I knew last night."

"How did you know?" I was surprised.

"Dad told me."

"Your father?" I said, a familiar feeling of fury and frustration rising in my throat.

"Yes, he said he was expecting you. That's why everything is ready." He looked round the room, checking

75

everything was as it should be, he was his father's son. "It *is* ready, isn't it?"

"Very ready," I said.

"He said it was to be made comfortable."

"That was thoughtful of your father. Almost too thoughtful."

Peter came into the room, looking about him with his eyes bright and a smile on his lips, as if he were happy. "He said you were to have that room overlooking the garden, but I said that was silly, it was much too grand, and that you always had this room. This is the room you like, isn't it?"

"Yes, this is the room I like."

"I think it's pleasant," said Peter, with that strangely adult air of his. "More homely."

"I shall have to thank your father."

"He's not here today. He went off again early this morning. He'll be back this evening."

"Does he often leave you alone?"

He flushed. "I'm not alone. You can't be alone in a place like St. John's."

I had forgotten how father and son felt about St. John's. And what he said was, in a way, true. The house had its own personality. I'm not sure if all of it was friendly, though. For instance, I always thought of the old part of the house as welcoming and the new part as essentially empty.

"I mean, I've got all my things about me, and there's so much to do," he said, anxious I shouldn't suspect him of any whimsy.

Jackson gave a squawk from his cage and attracted his attention. He went over. "He is a funny bird. But parrots usually are, anyway. I think they must have bigger brains than most birds." He tapped at Jackson's cage. "You know there's a story that the geese who saved the Roman Capitol by giving the alarm of attack were really just *one* parrot imitating geese."

"Where did you get that from?"

"From the *Feather and Wing Gazette*," he said gravely. Then he burst out laughing. "Go on, Anny, you believed me for a moment, say you did."

"I always believe you," I said.

"Yes, sure." His mirth at once melted away. "Everyone always does."

"Oh, Peter."

"No, sorry, Anna. I should apologise. I know you didn't mean anything. And I must learn not to be thin-skinned." I could hear his father's voice behind the phrase. "Back to where we were then, Anna? When we laughed?" It was him speaking now, with that spontaneous simplicity which always took my heart.

"Of course."

"In any case," he said gaily, with once again one of those lightning changes of mood, "I'm going away to be educated and be a good straightforward English boy. Whatever happened in the past, no one can touch me, there's a Statute of Limitations operating." He caught sight of my expression. "Oh, not a legal Statute of Limitations, that doesn't operate in homicide, does it?" I closed my eyes in pain. "But a moral one, because I was only a little boy then, and must be forgiven."

This was not his father's voice speaking through him this time. God knows where he'd learnt to talk like that. Someone had taught him; it didn't come out of his own nature.

"Peter," I said, deliberately speaking slowly. "You forget I was there when the accident happened. I know what took place."

"Virtually there," he said. "Not on the spot. Not watching. No one was. That was the point, don't you remember?" He gave me a little bow and went out of the room.

As he left me I could hear the sound of terrible music in my ears. Subtle, decadent music. I was convinced that someone, not his father, was influencing his mind, shaping him to this premature sophistication. When we had first met this time yesterday, in the wood, I had blamed the change in him on what had taken place in the past. I had accepted my own share of the responsibility for this. Perhaps I must still do so. But now I felt he was two people speaking, and one voice was acquired. He was two people, split down the middle like the house he lived in.

My hand went to my cheek. He could like me and dislike me at the same time, and never show the strain.

I started to put the few clothes I had brought with me on to hangers. A light blue tweed dress in case it turned colder. One or two silk jerseys, a tunic with pants to match, easy simple clothes. I had allowed myself one grand dress, what the French call *une robe de style,* because in this house you could never tell, I might need to wear it. In a drawer I put my second-best wig.

There was a small red leather box still to be disposed of. I opened it for a moment before looking for a hiding place. Inside was a pale watery aquamarine set as a ring. I always enjoyed looking at it, although my opportunities for wearing it were small. It had belonged to my grandmother and then been sold when she died and the family needed money. Now, it had come back into my possession. I put the ring box into a drawer and locked it. Its intrinsic value was, I suppose, as jewellery goes, not great, but it was mine and I loved it.

The telephone by the bed rang just as I had finished. It was Mrs. Twining from my own house.

"I've finished tidying up here. As far as I can, that is. You'll have to get a bit of repairs and painting done, but I reckon you could come back in a few days."

"I'll stay here for a bit."

"That's right, why don't you? Enjoy yourself." In the background I could hear an Elizabethan madrigal being sung. I wasn't sure what this choice of music told me of Mrs. Twining's mood. So far she had never been interested in any music earlier than Handel. Perhaps it was all she could tune in to. She soon enlightened me. "I'm reading a book about the Earl of Essex, Queen Elizabeth's boy friend. Of course, there was nothing much in *that,* you know, she couldn't, poor thing, any more than her sister Mary really could, it was all on account of their father. You know he had the most shocking . . ."

She was properly embarked on the medical history of the Tudors. I came back to hear her saying, "Fistula you could put your hand in," and I was glad I'd missed the bit in between. There was a pause and then I heard her say, "And I put your rose in water."

"What?"

"Your rose. It came as usual." She giggled. I wondered what she made of it all and what she thought I had been up to. She was a great romancer, though, and had probably built up quite a story of her own. I might get her to tell me one day.

"Take it home," I said. "I don't want it."

"One rose?" she said. "I mean, what's one rose? I don't think I've got a vase I could put *one* rose in."

"Wear it," I said. "Put it in your hat."

"I *could* wear it. I could wear it tonight. I'm going to a whist drive. I could wear it in my bosom." Mrs. Twining had a more than adequate bosom and she liked to wear a double row of pearls. "They'll all wonder where I got it from." The giggle again.

"Say you had it from your lover," I said, but I had put the receiver down by that time and I said the words to the open room. Not that Mrs. Twining mightn't have had a lover, because she prided herself on her advanced views, and had been an early subscriber to Women's Lib; but had she taken one, it would have been in a very experimental kind of way, and I don't suppose he'd have enjoyed it very much.

I went out of the room. The sunlight was pouring down through the great window which faced south-west. The staircase curved down to the hall. The staircase was genuine and had survived the holocaust as staircases will. The stone stairs were covered with a deep red carpet, which I knew had been woven specially for the house. It was a copy of the original designed and woven in Axminster in 1810, just as the great blue and white vase which stood at the bottom had been created by Josiah Wedgwood the first and sold in his new Piccadilly shop. This vase was genuine, having been carried out of the burning house by its owner, who then went back for his wife. That was how they thought of women in that house then: chattels first, wives second.

At the bottom of the stairs Peter was standing, looking up. I got the impression he was waiting for someone.

"Is your father back?" I asked.

"No." He sounded surprised. Perhaps he had been

79

waiting for me, then. He withdrew his eyes from the staircase and smiled at me. "No, I don't expect him yet, you know. I might not even see him. He comes and goes."

"That I know."

"I've got something for you."

"Have you?"

"Come and see, and I'll show you." He led me through a swing door towards the kitchen regions, you had to say regions in St. John's, they still used the huge old vaults that went back to the fifteenth century and had been occupied by the cooks and scullions of the knightly builders.

He went to a long baize-topped table and took off a crystal cup full of flowers. Red flowers, sweet and fragrant.

He held them out. "For your room."

"How lovely." I swallowed, I was having difficulty in speaking. "Roses, what made you think of roses?"

"You like roses, you know you do." He sounded puzzled. "We grow them here. You were picking them that day . . ." His voice trailed away.

"What day?"

"The day."

"I'd forgotten," I said softly. "Was I really?"

"It's not a thing I could forget," he said, with unexpected bitterness. "A thorn scratched your hand and there was blood on it. Dried by then, of course."

"I'll take the flowers up to my room." The tight feeling was still in my throat. I was still feeling unsure of him. I didn't know what his reasons were for giving me the red roses. I wasn't sure if I believed his story of the rose and the thorn. I thought he might be playing with symbols and allegories. I wasn't sure that the roses were meant for my pleasure.

"I'll take the flowers to my room," I repeated.

"Oh, let me," said Peter, politely.

"No." I needed to be alone to think. "Stay where you are. I'll be right back."

I put the flowers on my dressing table, where they were reflected in the mirror. I saw my own face above them, big-eyed and tense. It was an antique mirror and must have seen many wretched women. As I stood there, looking, the telephone by my bed rang again. I ignored it.

Then it stopped. A second passed, while I still stared at the roses, then there was a tap at the door.

"Anny?" It was Peter. "That's a telephone call for you. Will you take it?"

"No one knows I'm here," I said, deliberately obstructive, ignoring the fact that Mrs. Twining knew for a start.

"Don't be silly, Anny, it's Jean Driver." I could hear him running away down the stairs.

"Hello." I suppose I was still sounding hostile, as if I didn't want to talk.

"Hello, Anna, my dear."

"How did you know I was here?"

She paused then said, "Ben told me, dear, about your fire. And I was telephoning to see if you'd like to come over to a little lunch I'm having."

"Oh, no, thanks. I probably shan't bother with lunch today."

"Anna!"

"Well, I don't want to, Jean. I don't feel sociable."

"Just some of your friends, Anna."

"Particularly with my friends." Inside I was wondering who my friends were.

Jean said, with dignity, "Anna, I think it would be nice for your friends to see you."

I saw the purpose of the lunch then. I was being given protection by my friends. They were standing by me; I was not being shunned by them. They were showing they did not think me guilty of murder.

"And for you to see yours friends," said Jean, rubbing the point in. There was never anything very subtle about Jean, and I expect Ben had told her what he wanted her to do. She took a lot of notice of him.

"All right, I'll come over, and if anyone mentions the Marquise de Brinvilliers, I'll shoot them?"

"Who's she?" asked Jean, suspiciously. "Do I know her? I'm not asking her, anyway."

"No, Jean, you don't," I said. You couldn't expect Jean to have heard of a seventeenth-century lady poisoner, however famous.

As I dressed, I wondered what food Jean would have chosen for lunch, and who would have cooked it for her. You could never tell with Jean, sometimes she bothered with her food, at other times not. I find poor food depressing. But I dressed carefully in a plain rather superior trouser suit, which, I hoped, would make Jean envious. I had been saving it up to make someone envious.

As I approached the private service road into Jean's grounds I saw a car turning out of the gate. I recognised the driver. It was the policeman who had questioned me, James Dilke. I no longer thought he looked so agreeable and I certainly was not happy to see that he had now apparently already questioned at least one of my friends. There was nothing that Jean knew about me that anyone couldn't know, or so I thought. But many a fact has two handles on it, and if you pull one handle, it looks a harmless innocent fact, while if you pull the other, it has a question mark written on it. I didn't want Jean to start asking questions.

At the side of the house I saw a van with *Peter Pan Kitchen* printed on the side, so I knew who would be cooking my lunch, and I could even predict the menu. Salmon mousse, stuffed eggs, green salad, hot bread, fruit flan with whipped cream. This was their warm-weather menu. Good, plain, unimaginative food; but perhaps Jean would serve her own coffee. Under instruction from me, she had learnt to make quite decent coffee.

"Hello, Anny dear," said Jean, kissing my cheek. "Nice suit, I like it. Where did you get it?"

"Paris," I said. But of course, you can't impress Jean with words like Paris. She knows to a decimal point where she rates Paris in the scheme of things, and the exact degree to which Paris is, or is not, in tune with things this year. Words with hard centres like Gucci and Hermès and Wartski, words such as these impress Jean. This is what I call worldly.

The first person I saw, as I walked past Jean, was Lynn Alloway. The relationship between us was ambiguous. We had started off as employer and employee; then we had become suspect and accuser (with each of us playing

82

both rôles) and now, damn it, we seemed to have become friends. I swear she looked pleased to see me.

She advanced towards me with a glass in one hand and a cigarette in the other. "Nice to see you," she said. "Tim's feeling fine. Do you know, I think his little upset has really improved his health." There was a wicked glint in her eye. I thought, if I was Tim, I'd watch out.

"I hope he stays that way," I said.

"Oh, I think he will. Yes, I think he will. Tim's got a lot of resilience."

It was a small party, just Lynn and Jean and Dolly Compton and Rose, her daughter; I was interested to see that Jean regarded these as my friends. I did have other friends. There was Charlotte West, with whom I'd been at school and been close to until she married and went to live in Africa, and Ellie Batchelor, who was a dearer friend still, but who was at present in South America, following the habits of a remote and degenerate tribe of Indians and writing a book about them. But she'd be back soon, and so would Charlotte, and then I would have some friends of my own, instead of people I happened to live near.

No one mentioned poison, no one said anything about newspapers. Jean kept the conversation on the level she was best at, a sort of intellectualised prattle about books and films and people. She'd always read everything and seen everything and met everybody before the rest of us. Listen to her conversation, and you knew whose star was rising and whose day was over; she was marvellous at obituaries. If you didn't know her, you might think that her praise of this play and that boutique was a selling game, but when I heard her saying things like "Of course, I *love* that way of writing" or "You can always tell their clothes, can't you?" I knew her volatile admiration had moved on, and writer and shop were no longer for her.

Now she was talking about Ted and Eric and Vanessa. The names slid easily between her pearlised lips over the lobster mousse and Scotch on the rocks; she liked her liquor hard. You couldn't make the easy gibe that she hadn't really read the books she talked about, because she manifestly had, but she had read them with well manicured hands and it had been no effort to her. There should have been an effort, I felt deeply that the effort was what mattered.

Instinctively she must have responded to this in me, because she swivelled round and said, "Oh, come on, Anna, relax. You always take things so seriously. You're taking things seriously now."

"I always take food seriously, Jean, you ought to know that. I'm enjoying my lunch."

She beamed. She loved a compliment, even if an undeserved one, *especially* an undeserved one. I suppose the truth about Jean was she thought all compliments were justly hers. "It is good, isn't it?" She looked appraisingly at the lobster mousse. "You're not the only one who can cook, Anna."

"No, indeed, Jean." I suppose she thought I hadn't seen the van from Peter Pan at the door. I dare say, in some way, she thought she had cooked it. She'd paid for it, anyway, and with Jean it was, in the end, the dollar that counted.

"Have some wine." Jean poured it for me, a touch of concern in her voice. "You look a bit pale."

I sipped the wine and steadied myself. I wasn't usually so unpleasant about Jean. I knew her and saw what she was and still liked her. Or I had done in the past. Perhaps it was the presence of Lynn Alloway. There was something about her golden certainty that diminished me. Or perhaps I was just jealous.

No one mentioned my fire; I suppose they'd been warned to keep off the subject and be tactful. But there was one thing they had to touch upon and which obliquely dealt with all the others: St. John's.

"Nice to have St. John's open again," said Jean. "Has it changed much up there?"

"Not at all," I said.

"There's been a lot of decorating going on. I don't suppose one could tell the difference exactly, because with a house like St. John's redecoration just means keeping things looking exactly the way they always have done, no older but certainly no newer. But I've heard he's even claiming back some of the pictures the family loaned

84

to museums and art galleries. I think that's a little selfish."

"I don't see why he shouldn't look at his own pictures."

"I believe they are immensely valuable," said Jean, with respect.

"I saw him in Garrard's when I was in London," said Dolly. "I was getting a ring reset. I don't know what he was doing there, but it's not a place you expect to see Neil Despenser."

"I suppose they've got a few odd pieces of jewellery in the family. I've never heard they had much. Perhaps he is selling it."

"I think he's getting married again."

"No," said Jean with a giggle. "Not married. He's a real old Regency rake. Now that is in the family, if you like. I'm sorry, Anna, I know you adore him, and he's always been lovely to you, but the mercy is that he's never been attracted to you that way. But you know what he's like."

"I think he *is* getting married again," persisted Dolly Compton. "By all they say, the boy's quite odd, probably won't ever be quite normal now. He'd like another heir."

"They believe in primogeniture in that family," said Jean. "St. John's is entailed."

"Well," said Dolly, "perhaps the boy won't live long. I shouldn't be at all surprised."

Then she realised what she'd said and there was a poisoned silence.

"That's a lousy thing to say," I said.

"Of course, I didn't mean . . ." she began in a flutter. But she had meant it, and perhaps there was something in it.

"Say what you like. I don't believe in boy and girl marriages and that first marriage of Neil's was a disaster," observed Jean.

"She was ill," I said.

"There's very often an emotional reason for prolonged illness," said Jean sagely.

"She had rheumatic fever two months after Peter was born, it weakened her heart, and eventually she died," I said. "It could happen to anyone. To me. To you."

There was dead silence at this statement. In their hearts

they really thought a premature death was not to be associated with those who had a prosperous marriage, but was the punishment allotted to the unsuccessful.

They were too sophisticated to put this into speech, but all felt it.

At this point the waiter from Peter Pan wheeled in a trolley, and started to serve an iced pudding. He gave me a sideways look. I could imagine him going back into the kitchen and saying: She's in there, the one there's been all the talk about, I wouldn't like to share a meal with *her*. He put a decanter of white wine by my hand and defiantly I filled my glass. The wine was good and sweetish, Château Yquem, I thought. Jean had no inhibitions about expensive wines.

After I had finished the wine I noticed that the party had started playing their favourite game, which was *Dissecta Membra* or Fall on Your Friends. They were far too sophisticated to do it directly, but they had a number of ways of compiling a score. For the purposes of the game husbands could, under certain circumstances, count as friends. They were all, as far as I knew, and in their ways, happily married (Lynn Alloway excepted), but it was sometimes amusing to get a side swipe at a spouse.

They were talking now about a common friend, Ginevra, and Harry, her husband. I knew Ginevra. I don't think I'd ever met Harry, but the general impression was that Harry was a lamb who could be kitted out as a wolf on a suitable occasion, and that this was what Ginevra liked to do. She had told Jean that it made her feel good, and Jean told us that she could quite see why.

"I think it's creepy," said Dolly.

"No," said Jean. "But a dangerous way of getting kicks." Jean said it soberly, seriously, even kindly. That was the way of the game.

"Well, I'm sorry for Ginevra," said Dolly; she was usually the most forthright of them all.

"Yes, it's hard getting dumped at her age," said Lynn.

"I wouldn't call it that."

"What else would you call it? One day there'll be a new young wife for Harry and an empty home and a life of venom for Ginny: that's being dumped. I blame her;

she's built up a sort of image for Harry and in the end he'll have to live up to it."

"I wouldn't let him get away with it," said Lynn, easily.

"I think you're both wrong," said Jean. "It won't come to that. I think they're both having a hell of a time. You should see Ginny: she looks ten years younger. I expect Harry does too. It's the girl I fell sorry for. I expect she thinks Harry is absolutely genuine, and he isn't at all. He'll buy Ginny a new car and they'll have a holiday in Italy and it'll be marvellous. Ginny'll come back and tell us how marvellous it was. Then Ginny'll have another baby and *then* they'll start all over again."

Calm and judicious, she had it all summed up. In the game today her score was highest.

I put my hands over my eyes. I was a monster. These were my friends. I was distorting everything. When I opened my eyes I wanted to see everything as it had always been.

"Anna!" Jean was concerned. I could hear sympathy in every note of her voice. It was dribbling out. I was the next object for their sympathetic consideration. The game included me.

I opened my eyes and looked at them. I saw Jean. I saw Dolly, I saw Rose, her daughter. They were watching me, interested in my reactions. I wasn't *innocent* to them, only not yet guilty. They hadn't got me to this lunch party to protect me, but to have a look at me. Dolly dropped her eyes in an embarrassed way. Suddenly I wanted to do something violent, shout or stamp out of the room.

I started to get to my feet. Lynn Alloway touched my arm. "Don't," she said. "I know what you're thinking of doing, and don't."

"How do you know? How can you know?"

"Oh, surely," she said dryly. "Who better? We're standing here together."

"No one seriously suspects *you*."

"You do, for a start."

"I'm terribly frightened," I said.

"So?" She shrugged. "We all are. *They* are. They're frightened of you."

She saw the doubt on my face. "Oh yes, don't look surprised. You are dangerous. They don't understand you. For them that's dangerous."

"I'm easy to understand."

She looked long in my face. "Are you? You're very attractive. You look vulnerable, but you resist pressure. You've got something supporting you. What is it? A person? An idea?"

I shrugged.

"And as for our friends here," she went on, smiling at Jean, as if she wasn't talking about her, "they think you're not telling them all you could. You travel about a bit, don't you? Paris? London? They think you've got a secret and they wonder what it is. Is it the husband of one of them? Or are you a spy? One of them thinks you could be a spy."

"I'm surprised they said all that to you."

"They didn't actually say it. But they got it across. You see, you're ambiguous. Double-sided. And for them that means either sex or money."

"Each of them is three times as beautiful as I am," I said slowly.

"Ah. But you have a secret asset. Even if you don't know it yet." She had a wry way of talking that made even things she really meant sound like a joke.

"Some day I'll tell you about it. You'll be a big girl one day and I'll tell you."

Jean was smiling at me across the room. I went over to say goodbye. I'd known her a long time. I wanted very much to trust her. If only she'd be honest with me.

"Goodbye and thank you, Jean. It was a nice thought."

She gave me her usual warm soft handshake in farewell. Jean always had a special way of holding your hand, as if for ever. "I don't see nearly enough of you," she said.

"Well especially thanks for today," I said. "In view of everything."

"The fire wasn't too bad, was it?"

"I didn't mean just the fire."

A blank look spread across her face.

"You know what I mean," I said.

"No, dear, no, I don't. I have no idea what you are talking about." The warm handclasp fell away.

"Jean, I *saw* who was calling on you. I *saw* him."

"What are you talking about?"

"All right, Jean, if that's how you feel, I won't mention it again." I turned and walked quickly away. I knew now that I was really quite alone.

I drove back to St. John's, taking the road that did not pass my own house. I hoped Mrs. Twining was there, clearing up, but I had no wish to see. For the first time ever my spirits did not rise at the sight of the graceful white house. I drove round the back, to the old stables, and parked my car. Under the arch leading to the house where the grooms had lived I saw an unobtrusive Rolls parked. So Neil Despenser was back.

I went through the back door, I knew all the passages, into the hall, and up the big staircase. It was flooded with light and sweet with the smell of lilies growing in the big bowl at the turn of the stair.

I started to ascend. On the landing a girl was standing.

I looked up and she looked down on me. She was tall, with flowing tawny hair and a small oval face. She was wearing a dark green dress, cut close to her bodice, with long sleeves and a full skirt. Her red hair was crimped and full, her skin very white.

"Who are you?" I said, walking slowly up. Seen close to, her skin was fine and thin, her eyes a full dark blue with a black rim round the iris.

If she thought my manners bad she didn't say so. "Lily," she said, in a clear, sweet, unaccented voice. It was quite classless, she could have come from anywhere, any time. "Lily . . ."

"Lily?" I was incredulous. How could you come back so beautiful, I thought.

"Lily," she repeated. "Queen Lily and Rose in one. The red rose cries, 'She is near, she is near.' And the white rose weeps, 'She is late.' The larkspur listens, 'I hear, I hear.' And the lily whispers 'I wait.' " The words tripped off her lips and then, without saying anything further, but sending a smile backwards over her shoulder, she went silently on down the stairs and out into the garden. I walked on up to my room, left my things, then went to look for Peter.

I found him in his own sitting-room, quietly reading. About birds, no doubt.

"Is that Lily Madden?" I said.

"Oh, hello. Dad's back. He's in the Long Room." The Long Room was where they kept all their books: they carefully did not call it a library. He wasn't interested in Lily. He hardly remembered her.

"I know, I've seen his car. But *how* does Lily come to be here?"

He looked vague. "Think she came with the cook," he said, going back to his book.

I ran down the stairs and into the kitchen. A short, white-aproned woman was beating eggs in a copper bowl. There was a mixer and other modern equipment all round her, but she preferred the manual touch.

She knew who I was, for she gave me a warm smile, but did not stop in her beating.

"Got everything you want? I didn't have a look at your room myself but the boy said it was how you liked it. I'm Mrs. Mac. Maconochie, in fact, but Mac comes quicker."

"Everything's fine."

I went over to the sink, turned the tap till the water ran very cold, and filled a glass.

"They say that the water comes from a spring in the woods," said Mrs. Mac.

"I believe it does," I said absently.

"It tastes very sweet. You get a better cup of tea with such water. Of course, I'm lucky, I've always lived in houses where either the water was naturally good or you had Malvern water specially bottled for the tea and coffee."

"I've just seen your friend, Miss Madden," I said.

She continued her beating without a stop. "Not friend, miss. I've only just arrived. I haven't had time to make a friend yet."

"Oh? I beg your pardon. I mean the girl who came with you. She did come with you?"

"Not *with* me, miss. With me in the sense of accompanying me on the journey, yes, *with* me, no."

Her voice was cool and detached. She might even have been just a little offended at the suggestion that Lily was with her. I got the idea that she had reservations about Lily. So had I, for that matter.

"I thought you knew her," I said.

"We met at the railway station."

One day in St. John's, hardly that even, and the familiar feeling of exasperation and apprehension was rising in my throat. As always, it made me angry.

I put the glass down carefully, said goodbye to Mrs. Mac, and ran up the stairs. I threw open the door of the Long Room.

"Why the hell is Lily here?" I said to the man sitting writing at the round table in the middle of the room.

7

"My dear!" He came forward and kissed me lightly on each cheek. Always he had this formal courtly manner; it was strangely at variance with the rasp there often was in his words. I stood quite straight, accepting, even disregarding the embrace, which was, anyway, definitely impersonal. "How glad I am to see you."

"Yes. I know. I'm glad to see you. You look well." He did look well, a bit thinner than when I'd seen him last, but sun-tanned. "But why is Lily here?"

"I believe she's come to help with the gardens."

"She doesn't look like a gardener to me."

"She knows a great deal about flowers."

"She quoted Tennyson to me."

"I believe she's been quite well educated." He sounded amused. "Anyway, people usually remember bits of poetry with their name in it."

"So you've heard her, too?"

"Yes. Why are we talking about Lily?"

"Why indeed! I should have thought that was obvious." I flounced into a chair. I was behaving like a spoilt child and I knew it. In a way it was a wonderful relief to be able to do so. It was part of our relationship that I could vent my feelings and he would tolerate it.

"Lily's not important."

"She's beautiful. Anyone who looks like she does is important. Or going to be. Or has been."

"Yes." He looked at me reflectively. "I can see Lily does give that impression. She's led a relatively simple life, though."

"I hope she's not staying long."

"No, I don't think so. But she won't come your way much."

"Somehow I don't think you'll get her shut up in the kitchen with Mrs. Mac."

"No. I could hardly do that. But she's got her own set of rooms." You always had to remember when discussing Lily with Neil that there was a blood tie and with the Despensers blood, even when illegitimate, counted. After all, an early Despenser had been the bastard son of Henry II, that notorious womaniser. Old Sir James Madden was well known to be the son of Neil's great-grandfather who had been a bit like Henry II himself. The relationship had never been overly acknowledged but the boy had been well educated and had achieved success in life. With typical Despenser black humour he had come to live near St. John's. So Lily was a cousin beneath the blanket to Neil and had more right to live behind the iron gates with the Fleur-de-lys in them than I had.

"Oh? Where?"

"In the West Tower."

What they called the West Tower was simply a nineteenth-century wing of rooms, no more than six in all, built to house guests.

I nodded, satisfied. Lily would be separated from the rest of the house by a long corridor.

"Why can't she stay with her grandmother?"

"Would *you* stay with Lady Madden?"

"I've always thought she was very fond of Lily."

"She's a very tiresome old lady, as you well know, and not at all a suitable companion for a girl like Lily. She shouldn't have charge of her."

"She still needs someone in charge then?"

"They said at the clinic in Geneva that it was time she came out into the world again," said Neil briefly. "They don't believe in keeping people cloistered these days. Medicine's changing."

"But what can Lily *do*?" I said sceptically.

"She helps in the garden. She loves flowers. It's good therapy." He had his obstinate look on. "In the West Tower she has her own door to the gardens," he went on. "She can come and go as she likes."

"That'll be convenient for her," I said, my asperity not diminishing.

He saw it and smiled. "I'm glad to see you here," he said.

"And that's another thing: Peter said you *expected* me here."

"Well, I didn't plan it, if that's what you mean."

"Still, my room was ready," I said. I was in an obstinate, perverse mood and would have the pleasure of it.

He raised his eyebrows. "You've been staying in this house since you were seven. First with my mother and subsequently with me. My mother always called it your room. She said your mother always stayed in it before she married, and it was her room."

"And I miss *her*." Old Mrs. Despenser had been eighty when she died, and still beautiful, and not in any lavender and old lace kind of way either. Her chic had been essentially timeless, composed of elegant bones, thick hair, always well cut, and simple clothes. But you apprehended without need for conscious thought that it was a beauty that had not come cheaply and had been nourished by brilliant dressmakers and dedicated hair-dressers. There was nothing spoilt or cosseted about Mrs. Despenser, but she had never known the need to seek less than the best. This can give a great patina to a woman.

She had talked to me of my mother, whom I had hardly known. From her stories I saw that my mother had been pretty, determined and a little silly. But she had obviously been bubbling with vitality and Mrs. Despenser had resented the lethal virus that had doused this light for ever. Mind you, she had had to go to Warsaw to find that virus, a trip undertaken after a quarrel with her lover, and I suppose this was what I meant by her silliness. She could have stayed at home and remained

94

healthy. But I have to admit I had never missed her. She was gone before I ever got to know her. And I never nourished any fantasy stories, like some children, about the mother I might have had. Perhaps I knew in my heart that we were antipathetic and that she would have found my seriousness tiresome and I would have been irritated by her flightiness. (But she might have preserved my face from its scar. Old Mrs. Despenser would certainly have done so, but, by then, she was dead. Dying with her usual neat decorum, in bed and in her sleep.)

"You're very like your mother," said Neil, studying my face. "Did you know that? I found a photograph of her here the other day, taken when she was your age."

"She hated to be photographed."

"Yes, I know, nevertheless there is this one. Have you ever seen it?"

"No." I shook my head.

"I'll get it." He went over to a tall walnut cabinet, behind whose doors were many tiny drawers. Some of these drawers, as I knew, were fakes. You had to know your way about them to pick out the ones that opened. I watched him open a drawer and take out a small envelope.

He handed the envelope to me. It was a plain grey envelope of the type always used in this house. I opened it, and looked at the small photograph it contained.

"It's a snapshot, really," I said.

"Yes, I don't think your mother knew it was being taken."

I saw a round plump young face. It belonged to the sort of girl who had driven a sports car in the nineteen-thirties and learnt how to fly and been brave during the war. A girl who had worn square-shouldered boxy jackets and her hair long and curled at the ends. A girl who had danced and been courted in nightclubs and sunned herself on expensive beaches. These were all things I knew she had done.

"Why, she isn't pretty at all," I said, disappointed.

"She didn't photograph well. I think that's why she didn't like to be photographed. But it's there, if you look into the picture."

"Can I have the photograph?"

"Yes, if you want."

"She wouldn't have been so very old now," I said, looking at it again.

"Ten years older than me," he answered, not making it clear whether he thought this old or young.

"You admired her, didn't you?"

"We didn't meet very often." He went over and closed the doors of the cabinet and behind them all their secret drawers.

"I don't think she could have been a very happy person."

"Yes, she was, very. But in a way that couldn't have lasted. She needed health and vitality and youth to be happy."

I wondered if I'd inherited anything from my mother except her money. I couldn't make out if it was bad luck for her or good luck, dying when she did. I was inclined to think it was fortunate, in which case I had not inherited her luck.

"I'm still wondering about Lily," I said. "Naturally I don't believe all the gossip about you."

"Naturally."

"Because, as a matter of fact, I believe Jean and the other women rather enjoy the gossip and talking about you in that way and invent it for that reason. Still, Lily *is* very striking."

"Yes, that describes Lily. Would you call her more pretty than beautiful?"

"Beautiful," I said, without any hesitation. "Beautiful. As if she'd stepped out of a pre-Raphaelite portrait, that sort of beauty. She's like Lizzie Siddal or the Lady of Shalott."

"I've never thought they had very happy lives, and perhaps Lily hasn't either."

"Don't you *know*?"

"I don't know too much about Lily," he said slowly.

"No one has told me how long you are back for, except to drop hints that it's for a long time."

"For good, I think. I've made the decision."

So the hints were right. It was amazing how often

96

hints and suggestions about Neil Despenser had some truth in them.

"It's the right thing to do. I never thought you'd do it, though."

"I had a strong motive."

"Yes." I nodded. I felt I didn't want to know what that motive was. "You know about the fire in my house? Peter has told you?"

"I know." He didn't confirm that it was Peter, and perhaps it hadn't been. There were plenty of other willing voices.

"But you know, also, why I've really come? For shelter, I suppose you could call it. You know about the other thing—the children and the poison?"

"I've heard." He put out his hand and took my own in it.

"You know it wasn't really me?"

"I've heard that, too."

"Then you've only heard it from a select number of people. Perhaps only one. Ben, I suppose." He didn't correct me. "A lot of people wonder if I'm a poisoner. The police do, I'm sure."

"I doubt that."

"They sent a man to question me." I could feel my hands begin to tremble.

"*Did* they?"

"Yes, don't look so surprised. They were bound to turn to me. We tend to think here on our privileged little island in the woods that we're safe—safe from everything dangerous. But it's not so. I've learnt I'm not safe. I suppose that's why I've come here, taken refuge with you."

"I'm glad you have done."

"St. John's is the big house, you see, the *centre* of privilege. I'm safe here." I was shaking. "Relatively safe. Safer than outside, anyway. It's like the medieval peasant taking refuge in the baron's castle when the invaders came. It's the last manifestation of feudalism, vassalage. Like *droit de seigneur,* that's another one. Now you know about that, don't you? Or does Lily . . . ?"

His hand slapped me across my cheek, hard.

I stopped, the tumble of words ceasing to fall out of my mouth.

"Sit down."

I watched him go to a wall cupboard and take out a small decanter. He filled a glass.

"Drink it."

I did drink it. I dried my eyes and in spite of myself felt steadier. "What nice brandy. It has a special flavour."

"It's plum brandy," he said. "I think the plums give it a powerful uplift."

"Why didn't you let me have my fit of hysteria?" I rubbed my cheek. "I would have enjoyed it."

"That was beginning to be obvious."

"Yes. I suppose I ought to feel ashamed of myself. I don't, though. I feel much better."

"It's never good to bottle things up. And if you had to do it at all, I'm glad you did it in front of me."

"Yes. You've got a good line in slaps. I shouldn't wonder if there was a bruise."

"Go and dab your face with some of that expensive lotion you keep, and you won't have a bruise. Judging by the smell, it's mostly witch hazel; that'll take away the bruise."

"What a lot you know about herbs."

He smiled. "I expect you'd like me to say my grandmother was a witch, but in fact I learnt that one playing rugger."

"You forget," I said, dreamily, the brandy still playing its part, "that I knew your grandmother, too. Just. I just remember her when I was a little girl. I probably knew your godmother as well."

"What a lot you know about me, then."

"Not enough," I said. "Not nearly enough."

There was dead silence.

"You know everything important," he said. "Here, let me help you along to your room and you can lie down."

"Everything? Reported or real? There's a difference."

"You're talking rubbish," he said, his voice good-humoured. I resented the good humour.

"I can walk to my room myself," I said. "And what's more, I will."

"Very well," he said, sinking back into his chair before his desk. "You do it."

I lay on the little curving silk-covered sofa in my room and was quiet. I hadn't thought of myself as a person who lost control, but I had just come very close to it. And I felt splendid. Not wretched or self-conscious or exhausted, but refreshed.

Presently, there was a tap on the door, and Peter came in with a tray bearing a teapot and a cup and saucer.

"Dad thought you might fancy a cup of tea."

"Oh, you've brought the violet china," I said, picking up the delicate shell of Victorian porcelain painted with a shower of tiny violets.

"Thought you'd like it, I'm having a cup with you." He was pouring an amber stream into another cup—I suppose it was the good Himalayan tea that Mrs. Mac and Mrs. Franks had agreed upon. "Dad says it's too good to use, really, but we do use it, all the time."

"When I was little, I used to think you could smell the violets as you drank." I sniffed delicately at the side of the cup. "Nothing there now. I'm too old, I suppose." I sipped my tea. "You know," I said, "I'm not sure if your father really expected me here or not."

"Oh, it was me," said Peter, with a smile. "It was me made sure you'd come."

"Made sure?" Was that just an expression, or had he indeed "made sure"?

"What do you mean, Peter?" I asked. "Just hoped it would happen or really did something effective?"

"Oh no, not did anything. Just willed it and willed it, Anny." He smiled his brilliant, forgetful smile. He could be extraordinarily remote while being so affectionate. I almost felt as if I wasn't there at all.

He finished his tea in a gulp. "Goodbye, Anna, I must go now. I've got a bird in the garden I'm studying."

I poured myself another cup of tea and drank it slowly after Peter had gone. I had to admit that I felt more relaxed without him in the room. I wondered if his father really had sent me the tea, or if Peter had made that up too?

I lay back comfortably on the soft yellow pillow of the

couch. It would have been easy to drift to sleep. Through the open window I could hear the chatter of one of those birds Peter was studying. Otherwise there was no noise.

Just as my eyes closed I saw a little bit of paper sticking to the tray. It was placed there unobtrusively underneath the cream jug, rather in the way French waiters leave the bill for your café au lait.

Slowly I leaned forward and picked it up. It was a scrap of thin paper, about two inches by three. On it were neatly printed in pencil a few words:

WHAT ABOUT POISON FOR CATS?

I picked up the paper carefully. My first feeling had been to tear it into shreds, but I drew back from this. It might be in my own interests to preserve it. For the first time I had objective, concrete evidence that someone was taking an unconcealed interest in me. Whether the interest was friendly or hostile was a matter of interpretation. All I knew was it frightened me.

And then, who could have put the paper on the tray? There were so few candidates. The cook, Mrs. Franks, Lily, Neil Despenser, or Peter himself.

It can't be Peter, I thought, he loves me. And then I thought: but he doesn't love anyone, he no longer loves anyone at all. This is why his father has brought him home. He has seen this strange loss of emotion.

If you don't love, can you hate? I wasn't sure. But I did begin to wonder if, in seeking the protection of St. John's, I had not put myself into a position of greater danger.

8

I changed my dress and carried my tray down to the kitchen. I could hear voices, and at once recognised Mrs. Twining's carrying tones. I wasn't altogether surprised to hear her. I knew she had been longing to penetrate the fastnesses of St. John's and see for herself what was going on.

She was sitting at the kitchen table. Opposite her was Mrs. Mac, shelling peas. Mrs. Twining looked at me cheerfully.

"Dropped in to see you," she said. "I've brought your letters." She handed over a small pile, most of which I had already seen and which I knew and she knew to be only an excuse. "And I brought you a few more clothes, as you're making a stay."

"Am I?" I raised my eyebrows. I probably was if she said so, but it was nice to be clear.

"I thought so." She cast an appraising eye at the bowl of green peas. "How are you going to cook those? Small onions, lettuce, lots of butter?"

"Plain with mint," said Mrs. Mac tersely.

"Dull," said Mrs. Twining, screwing up her nose. "You've got to be broad-minded and use your imagination to cook."

"Three queens and two viceroys I've cooked for," said

Mrs. Mac. "So I ought to know something about cooking."

"Which queens?" said Mrs. Twining at once, seizing on the question I'd liked to have asked myself.

"When I entered their service, I made them a solemn promise I would never talk about my experiences in their households and I never will. But queens they were."

Mrs. Twining then went on without hesitation to the question which naturally arose next. "Do they pay well?"

Mrs. Mac ignored her and went on shelling peas. They were popping out like bullets from a machine gun but, I hope, softer. "I'm thankful I've always lived in big establishments with their own dairy produce," she said. "Eggs and butter and cream from their own farms."

"I don't like farm butter," said Mrs. Twining. "Tastes a bit strong for me. Rank. Cheesy. Makes you wonder if they've got their utensils quite clean."

I thought Mrs. Mac would burst. "You don't know the taste of good butter," she said.

"Did you come from somewhere like that to here?" I asked.

"No. I've been retired from royal service for some time now," said Mrs. Mac. "I've been living in Kensington."

"Here, these people you've worked for," said Mrs. Twining, thrusting on, "did they keep an eye on the bills? I mean did they *mind* what things cost? Were they mean?"

"They had people to do that sort of thing for them," said Mrs. Mac. "Bills didn't come their way."

"Lucky them," said Mrs. Twining with a giggle. "Well, I must go now, if I can't help you any more with these peas." Mrs. Mac gave a snort. "Shall I come up and see you again tomorrow, madam?"

"Yes, do," I said. Mrs. Twining had never called me madam. Dear or you was more like it. By the glitter in her eyes, I saw it was aimed at Mrs. Mac. "If you've got time."

"Oh, I've got time, I've dropped out of my evening classes for the time being. I found I wasn't really making much progress. One of those academic troughs, you know. So I thought, Edie, my dear, you need a rest."

I followed her out into the garden. "What did you really come for?" I said.

"Read me like a book, don't you? I came to see you to

102

tell you that that detective has been prowling round again. Interested in your fire, I suppose. Still, I thought you'd wish to know. And I wanted to tell you."

"Did he come into the house?"

"Yes. Came in. Spoke to me. Asked questions."

"What sort of questions?"

"Well, who called at the house, when were you out, when was the house empty."

"Did he ask where I was now?"

"No." She shook her head. "He was looking round him all the time. That was what he really came for, I think, to *look*."

"And did he look?"

"Well, he didn't do more than look. I didn't let him touch anything. I suppose he's honest."

I walked with her to the end of the garden, where she got on her bicycle. I felt strangely lost and lonely when her sturdy figure had disappeared out of sight, waving cheerfully. She was enjoying every moment of drama, no doubt about that, but on the other hand she seemed to be one of the few people who didn't think of me as a possible mass poisoner. In fact, she never even mentioned the subject. And yet I knew her well enough to grasp that in certain moods there was nothing she'd have enjoyed more than a real going over it all with me. It was good of her to hold back.

I didn't return to the house. The sight of the garden lying golden in the afternoon sun had suggested an idea to me. The idea was Lily. I thought a conversation with Lily, always provided you could have one, might produce some interesting results.

Some time later I was wondering if you could talk to Lily. I had discovered her, finally, working quietly away among the seedlings in one of the big greenhouses. A little to my surprise, she had not been easy to find. I had wandered round the big old-fashioned garden fruitlessly for some time. Even the Despensers couldn't keep this garden in the exact state of crisp tidiness for which it had been designed. But the slight disorder of the walks and alleys added to its romantic charm for me. It appeared a lost, delicious world. Nowhere could I see Lily, but it seemed to me that as I walked down one shady path I began to get glimpses of a green skirt whisking out of sight, and that she was indeed there and watching me all the time. So I went and sat down on an old grey stone seat and watched the sunlight in a pond lighting up the great golden fish sleeping in its depths, and let the sunlight move westward a little, and then I went and found her bending over a frame of little plants in a greenhouse which smelt of damp earth and sweet living greenery. Lily looked up and smiled.

"Hello," I said.

"Hello." There was earth on her fingers and a small leaf had caught itself up in the profusion of her red-gold hair. She looked wonderfully beautiful, but not quite of this world.

"I was looking for you."

She smiled without answering. If indeed I had been right and she had not only known I was there, looking for her, but had been at pains to evade me, then a smile was about the proper answer. It wouldn't do to underestimate Lily.

"I wanted to talk to you." I had already decided there was no point in not being, within reason, open to Lily. "I thought you saw me."

"No."

"I was walking down the paths by the lake and I thought I saw you looking at me."

"Oh?" It was barely a question, just an uninterested polite little monosyllable, as she turned back to her plants.

"Then it must have been someone else," I said, exasperated.

"Yes."

"Oh, so there *was* someone there?"

"Lily one. Or even Lily two," said Lily.

"Are there three of you then?"

"Three's too many," observed Lily.

"It's what you said."

"No, you," said Lily, putting her fingers deep in the soil, as though the contact gave her comfort.

And so I had, in a kind of way. "Oh, Lily," I said,

before I could stop myself. Her style of speech was catching.

"Nice little plants," said Lily, fingering one tiny green sprig gently. "Real true seedlings, building up a root system, not turning into corms or rhizomes." As she spoke she looked remote and even almost as if she was someone from a foreign planet who had somehow put on human guise. For the first time it struck me that she might be lonely. I had a strange mixture of feelings in my heart about Lily, but she was a girl of my own age and I was touched.

"Where do you feel at home, Lily?" I said softly. "Where's your home?"

"In the country," she said, straight away. "I've always lived in the country."

It was hard to take that literally; she didn't look altogether a country girl, she seemed so far from rustic.

"I suppose I've always lived in the country too," I said.

"Not this country," she said, looking at me with her great blue stare. "Foreign. I can tell."

I was surprised. I have foreign blood and I have lived abroad. I never think it shows. It was a sharp reaction for Lily and showed, I thought, that she had observed me and passed a judgment.

"I live here," I said firmly. "I have a house in the woods."

"I'm not so fond of woods," said Lily. She frowned. As she did so, I realised that she was somewhat older than I thought, not the seventeen or eighteen I had believed her, but older, nearer twenty-five.

"I suppose you can't grow seedlings so well there," I suggested.

"*That's* not the reason."

"I was only joking."

"You shouldn't joke." She pushed her hair away from her forehead, in a gesture I was already beginning to recognise as a sign of tension. "Not about the woods. The woods are dangerous . . ."

"Oh, I don't think so. They're peaceful, calm and beautiful."

"Greedy, dark and hateful," said Lily. "*You* ought to know."

"Me?"

Lily bent over her tiny plants devotedly. She eased one from its bed with her fingers, carried it delicately between forefinger and middle finger to a selected site, inserted it, and patted the earth gently down. Her nails were stained and black with earth. At the moment she looked like a creature that drew its strength from the soil. "Isn't it pretty?" she said. "Pretty, pretty thing."

"I can see you enjoy your job."

"Job?"

"Working here," I said. "Did you learn to do all this in Geneva?"

"It's true I am working here," she agreed, after apparently thinking it over. She ignored my question about Geneva. I had already observed that Lily lived intensely in the present. Perhaps this was what they had taught her to do in Geneva; they had given her a present and taken away the past.

"Yes, you are," I said briskly. "I suppose you're under some sort of contract to get the gardens stocked before you go?"

"Go?"

"Yes." I was even brisker. "Home."

There was a pause. "This is my home," said Lily, staring at me. "I live here now."

Back in the house, I wondered whether I believed Lily or not. In spite of her strangeness, I felt that she always spoke the truth, and yet in a very literal kind of way. It was very difficult indeed to know what to make of Lily, but I was trying and trying hard. I was disquieted by her arrival in St. John's. I was sure it meant trouble.

In a little while now it would be time to go downstairs and eat what would certainly be the excellent meal cooked by Mrs. Mac. I imagined that she would serve a good straightforward dinner, with nothing elaborate and no swagger, but every dish tasting absolutely genuine. In their cooking, as in all creative arts, people mirror themselves, and this was Mrs. Mac's style.

I was hungry for dinner and in a better mood than I would have credited myself with a short time ago. I walked into the dining room, but the large oval of mahogany was bare. Outside I met Mrs. Franks carrying a tray and looking excited.

"You're eating in the library tonight," she said.

I nodded. I knew that this room was often used when the family were alone. I went in and saw the round table in the shadow, with its silver and old-fashioned white damask gleaming in the light of the setting sun. There was a round bowl of red roses in the middle of the table.

I always loved the ease and generosity of this room, which was in the old part of the house, and compared it favourably in my mind with the oval drawing room, which had been reconstructed right down to every last Wedgwood medallion on the walls.

I saw that five places were laid.

"You have guests," I said to Neil Despenser, who entered then.

"Ben's coming," he said. "I thought you would like to see him."

"Oh." I considered this. In the past Ben and Neil had not been conspicuously friendly. They seemed to arouse a mutual aggressiveness in each other. Neil, being the older and more sophisticated, mostly managed to conceal it better, but I could usually tell. "You realise it will be the first time Peter has really met him since . . ." I hesitated. "Well, since."

"I do realise it. Yes. One way and another, he's done quite a lot of damage to you and to Peter, that young man, hasn't he?" He was carefully pouring sherry.

"It hasn't been his fault," I said at once.

"You're a good friend."

I wanted to deny this too, it didn't seem enough to call me Ben's friend, we had been so much more and so much less, but I couldn't find the right words.

I accepted my sherry, and took a long drink. I suppose it intoxicated me a little, or perhaps the plum brandy hadn't quite worn off. Carrying my glass, I went round the table.

"You," I said, pointing to one place set with silver and

with a small monogrammed silver cigarette dish beside it. "Cigarettes are death, but you still do it." I pointed again. "Me. And here's Peter. Ben opposite me. And here?" I looked up at him. "Lily?"

Neil Despenser merely sipped his sherry and looked at his watch.

"And Lily?" I said. "The Lily Maid of Astolat. If she is a maid, which I seriously doubt."

"Go on," he said.

"There's no going on. You have a perfect right to have Lily here."

"Yes, I do have."

"But I hope you'll look after her, that's all. She seems to me to be, well, not simple. Lily's not simple, but very very unsophisticated."

I was rewarded with a long cold look, Neil Despenser at his nastiest. "You can leave me to look after Lily."

"Like Peter," I said, and knew I had gone too far.

"Yes, like Peter," he said, giving me a furious look.

"I'd better pack up and go," I said.

"Go? Where to? Back to your incendiarist kitchen and all the little sick girls?"

"What a lot you do know about it, after all?" I cried, angry in my turn.

"I know about it? Of course, I do."

We were still there, angrily together, when Peter came in to dinner bearing a huge tureen of soup.

"Cock o' Leekie," he said cheerfully. "She made it specially for me. It's beautifully hot. Not as if you two look as if you need heating up. At it again, are you?"

"That's enough of that," said his father.

"Sorry, sir," said Peter, entirely unquelled. "I'll serve the soup, shall I?"

"We aren't all present," snapped his father, again looking at his watch. "Where is Ben Drummond?"

"His car's outside," said Peter. "I saw it."

"Then I wish he'd hurry up."

But it was Mrs. Mac who came in. "The doctor's been called away and can't stop. He sends his apologies."

"Who called him?"

"He didn't say."

108

"Well, he couldn't," said Peter to his father.

"Have you been talking to him?" said his father angrily.

"No. Of course not."

Mrs. Mac banged the door behind her as she left; I thought she was slightly deaf without knowing it herself, and didn't always hear what was said to her.

"It must be years since you've seen Ben properly," I said.

"I know what he looks like, anyway," said Peter.

"Yes, he hasn't changed." And it was true. Ben had been exactly what he was now five years ago or even seven. He was one of those people whose mould, as it were, sets early.

"Changed? No, I should think he hasn't," said Peter.

The meal proceeded slowly. Lily did not appear, and her host seemed, somewhat grimly, to have given her up. I was glad she wasn't there.

Nor could she have helped on the dinner table conversation, which was carried on largely between Peter and me, with an occasional acid addition from his father.

The soup was taken out. I had eaten and enjoyed mine. I had been hungry anyway, and I had found now, as earlier, that anger was bracing me. I had always had this lucky gift of thriving on tension.

A roast chicken appeared, smelling of tarragon, and accompanied by the dish of green peas.

After this we were offered a hot chocolate pudding. The menu was aimed directly at young male taste buds, Peter's, of course. I ate my way solemnly through it; it was very good.

"I did enjoy that," said Peter.

"Yes, Mrs. Mac seems to have judged your tastes very well."

"Oh, Mrs. Mac knows what I like," said Peter easily.

"Very clever of her to get on to it so quickly." I suppose I was slightly jealous. I had to admit she was levelling with me in my own game.

"Oh, she's cooked hundreds of meals for me in London," said Peter, then flushed pink and looked at his father.

No flicker of expression moved across Neil Despenser's

face; he might not have heard a word that his son had said. "Would you like some port?" And, seeing my expression, "No, I suppose not. It's not your drink, is it? I'll get some champagne up from the cellars tomorrow. We ought to have champagne, oughtn't we? To celebrate."

"I don't know what we'd celebrate," I said.

"Our being home, of course," said Neil, with a smile. "That *is* a cause for celebration?"

"Oh yes, of course," I said, smiling too, as if I hadn't noticed what Peter had said, his virtual admission that they had been back in England many months. Or, if not back in a settled kind of way, coming and going constantly enough to need many dinners and a place to cook and serve them in. In Kensington, I supposed.

I saw a glance pass between father and son.

They were liars, both of them. And I was caught up with them here in St. John's.

I knew that I had to get away, out of the house. Something unnatural and terrifying was happening. I could feel it all around me without being able to say where it emanated from.

On my bedroom table was a folded piece of writing paper. I don't know how it got there but the only possible deliverer was Mrs. Mac. Someone had turned back my bed, though, and drawn the curtains, so perhaps there was an unknown pair of hands at work in St. John's.

The writing was Ben's, and it said simply: "I'm sorry I couldn't stay. I need to see you and talk to you."

It was half-way between a command and a plea, just like Ben.

"Anything to get out of this house now," I thought. I put on a silk coat and moved quietly down the stairs. I could hear music coming from behind the big library doors and knew that this was where Peter and his father still were. They thought I had gone to bed early with a headache. Father and son had been sympathetic and polite but just faintly incredulous. Possibly I looked too healthy and had enjoyed my dinner too much.

I listened for a moment at the door. Music was pouring out all right. Mrs. Twining would have approved, they had on the *Trout Quintet* by Schubert, but I doubted if they were listening. Behind the music I could hear the counterpoint of voices. Mostly Peter, but an occasional note sounding from his father. They were using the music as a cover for talk.

I left by the big front door, which locked itself behind me. I was without a key, but I had no doubt of my ability to get myself back into the house. There were too many ways in, and I knew them all.

I took a path that swung to the west of the gardens; I meant to go to my own house first. The gardens were empty in the dusk and the greenhouses closed and dark. Wherever the elusive Lily was, she was not with her beloved seedlings. I suppose even she hardly sat up with them all night. I wondered if she had really been expected at the dinner tonight. It was rapidly becoming in memory a parody of the Mad Hatter's Tea Party, with places laid which nobody filled, and where each of us perpetually moved on from seat to seat. Conversationally, emotionally even, Peter, Neil and I had done just that, dirtied a plate and moved on.

I was approaching my house and wondering, belatedly, if I had my house key, when a hand gripped me from behind. I wrenched myself away. "What do you think you're doing?" I said irritably.

"I didn't mean to frighten you," said Ben.

"Well, you did. Or you would have if I hadn't smelt it was you."

"Smelt?" He sounded injured.

"You smell of cigarette smoke and disinfectant. I thought doctors had given up smoking."

"If that was the worst of my vices," he said, with a groan.

"From my point of view at the moment," said, rubbing my arm, "the worst is the way you grip people."

"I thought you might shout."

"There's no one about to hear, is there?"

"You can't tell in this place. Mrs. Twining has only just left. Before that old Lady Madden tried to call on you. Didn't seem to know you weren't home."

"It takes her a bit of time to learn some things," I said.

"Especially if she's drunk."

"Was she?"

"No, I don't think so, not tonight. Does she call on you often?"

"When she wants some money. She does at the moment. I must visit her and find out."

"Don't be too saintly," he said irritably.

I ignored him, as I often did when he was pettish. In the little wars between us I knew how to keep my end up.

"I'm not sorry for her, if that's what you mean," I said coldly. "One way and another I think we owe her something. Not me personally, but us here, all of us who live in this group of houses."

"She lost her grandson. That wasn't our fault."

"That's always been our formula, hasn't it? She lost her grandson, we say. We don't say that we think he's dead."

"We never found a body," he said slowly. "As far as we know there wasn't one."

"There were his clothes by the sea at the end of the peninsula. There was Peter in a state of shock. He said he didn't know anything. But he had been bathing. Both boys had been playing. We thought that there had been a fight, probably only a mimic struggle which perhaps took a more serious turn, and that Peter pushed the other boy under the water."

"He was seventeen. Years older than Peter."

"But he wasn't a heavy boy. He was thin and slight. We all decided it was physically possible. I know I did, even though I hated to think it. So his father took Peter away. That was the mistake he made. But we all helped him make it."

"You forget the letter from the Madden boy to his grandmother. He said he was sorry for all the trouble he'd caused and he was clearing out."

There was a pause, and then I said what had been gathering in my mind a long time. "I never thought he wrote that letter. Oh perhaps, for a minute at the time, I let myself think he did. But not for long. It was too easy. I believed one of us forged that letter. I believe that silently we have always acknowledged it."

"The police accepted the letter."

"They accepted it because old Lady Madden did."

"Well, there you are."

"She accepted it because we told her to." I said. "She believed us. And the police didn't know about the clothes or Peter or the bruise on Peter's face."

"So all these years that's what you've really believed and you've never said."

"I thought it was what we all believed tacitly. And, if you want my opinion, for what it's worth, I don't think old Lady Madden ever really believed in the letter. And that's why she keeps coming to me for money."

"Blackmail?"

I shrugged. "You can call it that. You can call it my guilty conscience if you like."

"I don't like the way all this is pouring out," said Ben.

"Surely you can see why? It's because it's not over. Whatever started then by the sea is still going on."

"You were least of all to blame," said Ben softly. "You were so very young."

"And yet it's me Peter seems to hate. Oh, perhaps that's too strong a word. He doesn't hate me, you, or anybody, but he never seems to forget."

"Forget what?"

"That we didn't trust him, that we didn't believe him when he said he didn't know anything at all about Robert Madden's disappearance."

"Should we have believed him, then?"

There was a pause while I gathered my thoughts. "Yes," I said, "I think we should have believed him."

Silently he walked on. "My house or yours?" I said, as we approached my own front door.

"Oh, yours," said Ben irritably. "It's nearer."

The door opened easily. Mrs. Twining had cleaned up well, but there was still a faint smell of smoke. I would have to get the decorators in. If I was still living in this house. My future seemed wide open. Once I had thought to myself I could have predicted where it was leading. Now, who could tell?

"Well," I said to Ben. "What was it you wanted to

talk about? Why weren't you at dinner tonight? You were expected. I didn't believe that story about a patient."

"Did Despenser?"

"I don't know. Probably not. Why?"

"I felt like cutting his throat."

"Oh, come on, now. I've told you before about letting your temper run away with you."

"I'm jealous of him."

"That's not a very good reason for wanting to kill him."

"It's him or me, I think, Anna?" his voice was questioning.

"You're wrong there." I was deliberately tough. "So that's why you wouldn't stay to dinner?"

"Yes."

"What an impetuous person you are, Ben, in spite of your professional training."

"I had another reason too." He sounded worried. "I wanted to talk to you, to tell you something, and I felt I just couldn't sit there, spooning up their soup and keeping it all back."

"As bad as that?"

"Yes. Much as I hate you being there, stay safe at St. John's, will you, Anna? There's bad feeling around. That fire you had might not be an isolated incident."

"I don't see myself as an object of public attack, somehow."

"What do you mean?"

"I feel under attack all right, but I wish I knew where it was coming from. I feel it's close in somehow."

"But I've told you, Anna, these people think you've been poisoning children."

"But I *haven't*, Ben," I said. "So who's been arranging to make it look as though I did?"

"You're safe at St. John's for the moment, I think," he said. "But I won't visit you there. You understand that? Come to me if you want me, but I can't ever come there."

Ben could be very emotional. I did wonder sometimes what sort of a doctor it made him.

"Yes, I understand," I said.

"Will you marry me, Anna?" he said softly, as we prepared to leave.

"No, Ben," I said. But I let him kiss me. The kiss must have given him courage because, his voice muffled, he said, "There's something that very much worries me, Anna. Something about your house at the time of the fire. The back door was wedged from the inside, Anna." He didn't look at me. "I wondered if you could think how that could have happened?"

"No, Ben," I said once again, my voice still more gentle than before; but a little trickle of cold misery ran down me.

So one more friend had half-deserted me. Ben thought it was just possible I had wedged the door myself. Plainly he must also be wondering if I had planned and achieved my fire myself too.

He was on the way to thinking I had indeed poisoned the children.

I felt as though he had given me a bloody nose, the more so because I guessed he was terribly unhappy at his suspicions. Surely, this had been his real reason for not wanting to join us at dinner, and for his plea to talk to me tonight and alone. Whether he admitted it to himself or not, he was wanting assurance of my innocence from me.

I wondered what he would have felt if I had accepted his offer of marriage?

I came back to the moment, to find Ben staring at me in a puzzled way. "You haven't been listening to me," he said.

"Yes, I have. You asked me to marry you and I said no. You expected me to say no."

He didn't deny it. "You ought to do it, though," he said doggedly. "I could look after you."

"I'll be all right." I said suddenly determined that I would look after myself and be beholden to no one. Not him, at any rate.

"Shut up and listen," said Ben. "I'm thinking of leaving here. Emigrating to Canada or the States. I haven't made my mind up yet. I'll see where I get the best offer. I wanted you to know."

"You'd leave here?"

"Yes. I don't think it's been a good place here lately. I haven't been happy. You must have noticed that."

"I had noticed something," I admitted.

"I'm ambitious, you know, and, somehow, it's never come off here."

"I know." I had sensed the frustration in Ben. He wasn't cut out to be the sort of quiet country doctor his father had been. His father had somehow been a great man with it. Ben rested in his shadow.

"I want my freedom," he said, under his breath and to himself.

"It's a good thing you haven't got a wife," I said, half amused, half pained.

"You'd be part of my freedom, Anny," he said, taking my hand. But I knew better.

I made an excuse and stayed behind in my house when he had gone. He didn't want to leave me alone there, but I had my own way.

"I want to get a few more things to take up to St. John's," I said to him. It wasn't true. I had a purpose in staying, but this was not it.

I let Ben out and went back into my sitting-room and then I stood there, looking about me.

If the policeman had been here looking around, it behoved me, I thought, to have a look round too. There might be something to find. And it seemed to me that it would be a good idea for me to find it before he did.

I was standing there when I heard a noise. A little creeping noise. Then a cough.

"It's only me, dear," said an old voice apologetically.

"Lady Madden!" I said.

"I've been sitting here waiting in the next room. Ever so quiet."

"All the time?" She'd been listening to every word, I expect.

"I dropped off, my dear. I crept in to wait when your Mrs. Twining was here. I knew you'd be back. And then I nodded off. Tired, you see."

Drunk, I thought. But she was fairly sober now. Or

even completely so. Except that to me she never seemed completely drunk or completely sober.

"I'm surprised Mrs. Twining didn't notice you."

"I didn't wish she should. I still have *some* pride."

"Too much," I said, looking at her thin figure made round and falsely cosy looking with its layers of jerseys and cardigans, finished off with floating chiffon scarves and pearl necklaces. The scarves were from Liberty's and one or two of the necklaces might be genuine, for all I knew.

"You've always been very good to me, my dear, and I appreciate it. You do it so nicely too. Tactfully."

"Ah, well, yes . . ." I looked around for my handbag. I had cashed a cheque recently and could give her some money this moment. She saw me looking.

"I haven't come for that this time. No. I've had a letter." She was holding out a square envelope. "Here, have a look. Go on, I want you to. I want your advice."

I knew who the letter was from; I recognised the writing. It was from Neil Despenser.

"He wants you to visit him," I said, raising my head from the letter.

"Yes, wants me to see m'grand-daughter. Shall I go? They haven't exactly been a lucky family for me."

"I think you should go. He might be thinking of helping you."

"Oh well, as to that, he *has* been helping me, my dear, for years."

"I never knew that." She was a secretive old thing.

"It was private. Personal. Anyway, he asked me not to speak. Didn't want it said he was *paying* me, you see. It was all done through lawyers."

"I understand. Anyway, you'd like to see Lily, wouldn't you?"

"Yes." She sounded doubtful. I sympathised with her. After all, Ophelia's relations must have found her chilling company and there certainly was a drowned, Ophelia-like quality to Lily. "Neil Despenser's never been anxious to see me much before."

"Only now he is."

"Yes, and that's what's worrying me. Should I go?"

"Why shouldn't you go?" I said, watching her expression.

She shrugged. "Well, you hear things, don't you? I've heard he's going to get married again. Might not suit him to go on paying my little pension."

I hesitated. Then I said, "I don't think marriage would interfere with that."

"Honestly? Still, I'm uneasy. Why start getting sociable? I don't think this is a lucky time of the year."

"I'm beginning to think that myself."

"The truth is, my dear, I'm a little afraid of Neil Despenser. Once, I wouldn't have been, but now I am." Her face looked drawn beneath its brave make-up, and I remembered what it was so easy to forget with her, that she was really a very old woman. "You know, once, when Sir William was alive and I was the mistress of a large household, I would have met Neil Despenser on equal terms. Now he's too much for me."

"And not for you alone," I said.

"*You* don't need to fear him, my dear child, you have so many weapons."

"So has he," I observed with feeling, but she was far away in the past.

"Do you know I once had eleven servants? All Chinese, of course. They make marvellous servants, so efficient and loyal. You have to let them have their little bits of 'squeeze,' of course, but if you let them keep that for themselves they do protect you from anyone else's depredation. I don't suppose Chairman Mao has stopped *that,* I mean, you couldn't do it, my dear, it's character. Character," she repeated dreamily. "They think of their civilisation as having ten thousand years of life."

Perhaps it was just as well she and Lily were not going to be together much: Lady Madden all past and Lily all present, their life-lines would never touch. Then Lady Madden came back to reality.

"Of course, Neil *may* be thinking the same sort of thing about me," she said. "I quite see from his point of view I'm hardly a stable character." She gave a faint

118

mocking giggle; in some ways she was an alarmingly acute old lady.

"Do you know a woman called Lynn Alloway?" I asked. It would be interesting to have her opinion of Lynn.

"It so happens we haven't met," said Lady Madden with dignity. "But I'll keep my eyes open for her."

"Yes, you do that." Suddenly it seemed a good idea. She did have a knack of picking up underground information. I had seen it in operation before. I would have an eccentric and not too reliable detective on my side.

"*You* don't believe I'll do anything, do you?" She gave a high hoot of laughter, which made me realise what an unstable ally I had created.

"Don't do anything dangerous," I said.

I saw her out of the door, thinking to myself that she was really a little bit cracked, and wondering if she wasn't dangerous—to me, of course. I took it for granted that she had done all the damage she could to herself years ago.

This time I locked the doors and drew the curtains before returning to my search.

I didn't search for long. This time I went straight to my hat box. I am old-fashioned or rich enough to have a hat box. I knew what I should find. I don't know why I hadn't looked in the hat box before. But now I knew what I should find before I had the lid off. I don't believe in precognition or anything, but I knew what I should see, what I should put my hand on. And there it was.

A bottle, with a cork in it, a crumpled rag that looked like a torn handkerchief, and a small white packet with the label POISON FOR CATS. Both bottle and packet were empty.

So there it was, my little treasure trove, white and passive, like a load of rats.

I put the lid back on the hat box. Then I put the box back on the shelf where I kept my handbags and locked the door. This was by no means my answer to the problem the contents of the hat box posed but for the moment it would have to do.

I put the key in my pocket, went into my sitting-room,

and put some Wagner on the record player. The *Siegfried Idyll* to be precise. Wagner clears the mind wonderfully. I sat and listened.

On an impulse, or perhaps because Wagner had indeed had a beneficial effect, I got up and prepared to leave. It was not late, not too early to go visiting. I was going to see the Alloways.

Lynn herself opened the door, looking her Botticelli best in a long straight flowery dress with floating sleeves. I thought I'd like to get her and Lily into one room together, and see who won.

"Hello," she said, in a friendly fashion. "Come about that dinner you're going to cook for me?"

"It would be nice to talk over one or two details," I said cautiously. Such as what exactly are your motives in giving this meal and asking me to cook for it? Such as who pays what indemnity if someone or everyone at this party takes poison? Who will be watching whose hand?

Tim Alloway was inside, sitting in a chair which looked out over the garden. He looked as if he'd taken a beating, and so, one way and another, he had. Lynn was smiling at him. She looked exuberant, life was running over and to spare in her. But I had the uneasy feeling that it was Tim who had given her the transfusion, contributing his blood to her life stream without even knowing it.

"Hello," he said, rising politely. Lynn pushed him back into the chair, "Rest, love," she said. He gave her an apprehensive look. I had second thoughts: Tim was not ignorant of what he had been obliged to offer up to his wife.

On the contrary, he was nervous he might be required to do it again. Looking at Lynn, I thought she was indeed a girl who might be building up a blood bank all her own.

"We were just having a lovely quiet home evening," said Lynn. "Weren't we, Tim darling?"

"Yes," said Tim gloomily.

"And I'm terribly happy because Tim has just given me the most lovely jewel."

Only Lynn would say "jewel" like that, instead of ring or brooch or ear-ring. It was the precious heart of her ornament that meant so much to her.

In this case it was a ring. A platinum band with a huge glittering mass set in the middle.

"Isn't it lovely? I've always wanted something as big as this emerald, it's huge, isn't it?"

"They don't come any bigger," I agreed. Or anyway, not often.

"Thank goodness," said Tim. "Or she'd want one."

I was glad to hear him speak and know that the old Tim wasn't quite dead. It wasn't inconceivable that he might one day bite the slender hand that bore that lovely ring.

"Come and have a drink." Lynn pattered over to the table in her Italian sandals and came back with an opened bottle of champagne. "Champagne's the stuff for emeralds and diamonds and summer nights." She poured me a glass. "What's it like up at the Big House?" There was a light mockery in her voice. "But it's your second home, isn't it?"

She didn't wait for an answer, but was fluttering round the room, getting herself a drink (she'd had plenty already), lighting a cigarette, and giving an appreciative sniff at the bowl of clove pinks on the table.

"I love these warm summer nights, don't you?" she said.

"If you want me to cook a dinner for you I will," I said slowly. "So long as it doesn't make you nervous."

"Oh no, I've already told you."

"Or your guests."

"I shall choose them very, very carefully for their brave hearts and sound digestions," she assured me.

I laughed. I really had to. Lynn was unbeatable.

"I don't mean I'm going to poison them," I said. "But I do seem to be a sort of catalyst. Poison seems to spring up around me."

"Tim doesn't think for one minute that you poisoned him," said Lynn. "Do you, darling?"

"No," said Tim, on cue.

"And I'll tell you something else: he doesn't think I did either. Do you, darling?"

"No," said Tim.

"And I'll tell you something," I said. "I don't think you did, either."

"I wondered about that," said Lynn.

We looked at each other.

"Well, we've established something," I said.

"Have we?" It wouldn't do to underrate Lynn's intelligence. Her eyes were as bright as a bird's. Still, she couldn't know what I knew. She hadn't seen the photograph in the book, the faded postcard; she hadn't read about a woman called Florence Maybrick.

"I think so," I said. No, she hadn't seen the things I had seen, but it came to me then that perhaps she had seen other things. Perhaps she had seen the photograph of a young girl, looked at a street map of a sleepy market town, seen the drawing of an old fashioned apothecary's shop. Perhaps this had been provided for her titillation.

The thought did not come fully developed into my mind. As I looked at Lynn then it was in embryo, already existing in all its essentials but not yet fully grown.

"Thanks for listening to me," I said, getting up to leave. Tim politely got up, too. We all walked towards the door. They had the floodlights on in the garden and it looked like a stage set, but empty, and waiting for the play to begin.

Perhaps Tim felt this, because he reached out and flicked off a switch. The garden was dead. Lynn gave a little cry of disappointment but Tim didn't put the lights back on again. I think I was glad that Lynn wasn't going to get it all her own way.

"We never settled anything about the dinner I'm to cook."

"Well, we *could* have exactly what we had before," said Lynn. "But on second thoughts I think I'll leave it all to you. We shall be about ten, I think."

Tim looked around at the summer darkness. There was no moon and outside the reach of the house lights the trees and bushes were sinister.

"I'll drive you back to St. John's," he said.

"The road is lighted."

"I'll drive you," he said firmly.

I sat beside him as he drove. I wondered what it felt

like to have been almost murdered. And then it occurred to me that I knew. It was what was happening to me.

Slowly and quietly the process was under way: I was half way to being murdered.

9

It's strange, feeling you are a victim and not being sure where the attack is coming from. I was certain of nothing except that I was under a threat. You couldn't mistake the signs.

"Drop me off by the big gates," I said to Tim Alloway. "I can walk the last bit. I'll be all right."

"Are you sure?"

"Yes. I'm quite sure." I suddenly knew I didn't want Tim Alloway driving me, in that flashy car of his, up to the door of St. John's.

I had dressed myself to meet Lily and the long silk skirt hampered me and slowed my footsteps. All the same, I made good speed up the long path to the house. There was enough light to see by, but only just. I walked in the middle of the path, keeping well away from the trees and bushes.

Never run when you are frightened, it only invites pursuit. I had learnt this rule, so I didn't run. But I kept my head down and walked fast. It was ridiculous; there could be no one following me. The manner in which the bushes leaned and swayed and creaked was due to the light wind that was rising. I was wearing a long cloak over my dress and I hugged it about me, drawing the hood up over my head.

I thought I heard a light hissing noise coming from the lilac bushes on my left. I looked round, but nothing was there, only leaves moving in the breeze. I hurried on.

I knew I couldn't get into St. John's quietly through the front door, which had locked itself behind me. I could ring the bell or wield the great knocker and be let in, but if I wanted to return unobtrusively I had to find another entrance. I knew at least three. Since childhood Ben and I and no doubt Peter too had known all the unofficial ways into the great house. The simplest was a narrow window on the ground floor by the kitchen which, as long as I had known it, had never been successfully locked. You could always open it. But if that window no longer opened at a touch I knew of two others that would.

I could see lights behind windows up and down the facade of St. John's but round the back by the kitchens it was darker. I found my window and it opened obligingly to let me in. I slid through and into a quiet back passage. I knew if I followed it I would come out into the great hall near the foot of the staircase.

I stood there for a moment, getting my breath back. I felt safer now I was inside St. John's. Hardly a rational reaction really, when you remember that I strongly suspected the inhabitants of being, at the very least, liars.

I walked forward slowly. The scar on my face was beginning to burn. I knew this for a bad sign. Soon it would be red and glowing, dividing my cheek and my heart in two.

I was used to being two people but it wasn't healthy or particularly honest. I was a liar in my way, too. There were plenty of people who believed things about me that were false. Or if they didn't believe them it wasn't my fault: I had certainly made every attempt to see they did.

Without really being conscious of my action, I drew my hood closer about my face, covering my cheek.

The corridor itself was dark but I could see the lighted great hall at the end of it. I could even hear faint strains of music, which told me that Neil and Peter must still be in the library.

Suddenly a figure, heavily dressing-gowned but unmistakable, appeared at a door on the left leading, as I remembered, to what used to be called "the servants' hall."

"Lily," said Mrs. Mac's voice in a low whisper. "Is that you, my girl?"

I hesitated, not saying anything.

"Because if it is then I have to tell you I don't like you gallivanting round in corridors late at night."

I was about to speak but she swept on.

"I may be old-fashioned, indeed, I know I am, but in my opinion this isn't the way to get yourself a husband. You're a foolish girl. Now, Lily my dear, it's not a question of morals or anything but of plain good sense. Is it policy now?"

It was going to be awkward now to tell her who I was.

"Go away with you upstairs and make yourself respectable. You look quite a gawk in that get-up."

She was saying much more than she'd have done if she could see my face. The darkness emboldened her. I did try to stop her, but she *was* a little deaf and didn't hear me.

"And then, you see, my dear, he's not reliable. You canna trust him. You shouldn't, indeed, Lily, or where will you find yourself? I've only been here such a short time myself but I'm hearing the stories . . ."

But she had gone on too long, the library door opened, music and light flooded out. Mrs. Mac shrank back into the servants' hall with an exclamation, and I hurried forward. I think she hadn't seen my face; she still thought I was Lily.

My hood fell back round my shoulders. The stairs were near, but I couldn't get up them. I was fairly caught.

"Well," said Neil. "Little Red Riding Hood in person, caught by the Wolf Rampant. Where have you been?"

"It's beginning to rain," I said.

"I know that. Where have you been?"

"Just out." I was anxious to escape up the stairs before I said something unforgivable. Although between us, as matters now stood, I didn't know what was unforgivable and what not.

"A little midnight walk?"

"It's not midnight."

"Not far off. I don't like the idea of you wandering around late at night on your own." He gave me a look. "If you were on your own."

I laughed.

"You're angry about something."

"No." I halted at the foot of the stairs. "I feel you've made a fool of me."

"Surely not? That's something you can only do to yourself." He had a nasty way of putting things, but I had asked for it.

"All right. That's what I mean, then. You've helped me to make a fool of myself."

"If I did do that, then you are right to be angry," he said.

"You don't deny that you and Peter have been in England, in London, very much more than you have allowed me to believe. You let me think that you were staying in Paris for Peter's sake. It hasn't been true; for reasons of your own you have had a base in London." My anger was increasing with every word. "You taught me to think I was being helpful to you and your son in coming to Paris and being with you as I have. More than that, you made me think I was important to you. I see now I was not. You simply made use of me. You've been lying to me all down the line."

"What a wicked tongue you have. You've kept that hidden until now."

"Now *you* are learning something," I said.

"It doesn't put me off, you know." He sounded amused.

I had turned to face him, and, since I had by now got up several stairs, this brought our faces about level.

It seemed inevitable and almost natural that we should kiss.

I turned and began to hurry on up the stairs.

"Don't forget, champagne supper tomorrow night," said Neil softly.

He was older than me. I had known and quarrelled with him most of my life; I thought he was a liar, and I strongly suspected his son of being, at least, an agent of some of my misfortunes, and yet I not only allowed the kiss to happen, you could say I provoked it.

Sex, I thought, bloody bloody sex. I was furious with myself.

I saw Peter standing by his bedroom door. I suppose he'd heard his father and me talking. Perhaps I'd been shouting, although I don't think so. I stopped.

"Peter, have you been trying to hurt me? Do you hate me very much? Would you want to hurt me?"

He drew back. "No, Anny, of course not. I don't know what you mean." His attitude suggested that here was nothing but another piece of adult unreason.

"All right." I was very weary.

"You've been good to me. Coming over to Paris, staying, making things homely, helping me there."

"Perhaps you like me in Paris and hate me at home."

"Anny, I'm not quite crackers." He sounded alarmed, as if he was really saying: Anny, are *you* mad?

"All right, all right. Go to bed now. I'm going."

"I can't sleep. Dad keeps playing music so loud I can hear it in my room."

"Tell him to stop, then."

In the silence and peace of my own room I reflected how little I seemed to know of father and son. I had the feeling that there was a puppet master, and Peter and I were prominent among the puppets.

Peter had been back in England more than I had understood. He had a good deal of freedom; he would not find it difficult to come and go.

It wasn't easy to fit him into the picture made by the poison appearing in the children's sweets and Tim Alloway's food and drink. I had to admit I didn't see this clear and straight. All I had was suspicion and an uneasy feeling that only someone close to me would have desired, or *needed* to involve me in this way. You have to know someone very well to hate them in the way I appeared to be hated.

On the other hand, the fire in my kitchen, the anonymous note calling my attention to "poison for cats," the secreting of a bottle and a packet labeled POISON in my hat box where no poison had been before, this was something again.

128

"Those are child's tricks," I said to myself as I lay wide-eyed and sleepless in bed.

In his cage by the window I heard Jackson give a subdued squawk. He wasn't sleeping either. In spite of myself, I yawned.

I woke up to blue skies and sun filling my room. I got up quickly and dressed in trousers and a shirt. It was going to be a working day.

I was standing in the big immaculate kitchen, drinking some coffee, when Mrs. Mac came in.

"Oh, so you're here," she said. "I was looking for you. There's a man wants to see you."

"So early?"

"It's past nine o'clock."

I didn't ask her who this man was; I knew it was the detective, James Dilke. I suppose, in a way, I'd been waiting for him to call and ask for me, I'd had the same feeling you get when you know bad luck is coming.

"Is he coming here?"

"He's here *now*."

I finished my coffee with deliberation. I could see Mrs. Mac watching me curiously.

"He's a policeman," I said, just to keep her happy.

"Really?"

"Yes. One of my brilliant little circle of friends." I prepared to go. I could see she was watching me still, with that strange questioning look I had noticed before. It came to me that she knew something.

"Do you know him? Have you met him before?" I seized her wrist. "Please tell me."

"Yes, once." She pulled her wrist away. "My, you've got a grip on you, miss."

"When did you see him?"

"Well, you know . . ." She looked at me hopefully, as if I might save her the labour of elucidation.

"No, I don't know."

"He visited."

"He came to see *you*?"

"Not me. I saw him. I think Mr. Despenser knows him."

129

Oh yes, I thought. Neil Despenser knows him, I'm sure. Fatal, treacherous Despensers.

James Dilke was waiting outside, beside his neat official-looking car. I saw he was his own driver. Discretion, I supposed.

I stood there, looking at him. He had the gift of appearing to you just as you remembered him. Some people change in the mind until you hardly know them when you see them again. Neil Despenser was such a person. But this man was not. Here he was, just as he had been the other day. Perhaps you call that integrity.

"Where shall we go?" I said, without preamble.

"Your house?"

"No. Let's get in the car and drive."

He got in silently and I, equally silently, got in beside him. "Just drive," I said.

For a minute or two we drove. "Turn here," I said, "and take the left turn. There's a road straight to the beach."

The road took us through the deepest part of the woods, where they were greenest and darkest. There are some moods in which I find the woods hateful. Now, I closed my eyes as we went through, but I could feel the trees on either side of me reaching out and almost touching the car.

The car stopped. "We can talk here."

"No." I looked about me. "Not here."

"It's peaceful."

"Yes, it's the heart of the wood, It's the part they call Ironwood." He had, above all, the ability to make you put into words things you would rather not say. Now I had told him about Ironwood.

"And a part you don't like?"

"It's gloomy. There's the remains of a settlement where early iron smelting was done. Primitive iron smelting was often done in a wood or forest because of the trees for fuel. Of course, it's all overgrown and long forgotten, but I don't like the feel of it."

"Not because of the history, though," he said. "Something happened there once that you'd rather not remember, didn't it?"

130

So many things had happened in the woods, we had played and gossiped and quarrelled there as we grew up. The woods were full of ghosts.

"What is it?" he asked. "Tell me. What troubles you?"

"It's not easy." And yet it should have been easy, really, but I was reluctant to put things into words. Our childhood life in the woods seemed a sort of idyll. An idyll that went wrong. A cliché, but behind every cliché is a hard little truth with an old face. "We played games, we had picnics, we watched the animals and made them our friends, only . . ." I hesitated, then went on, "Slowly, I realised that the others had games and quarrels in which I did not join. I was younger, you see. I began to feel that the older ones, Ben and Lily and her brother, had secrets that I and Peter, even more, didn't share. It was silly, really, all it meant was that they were growing up and I was still a child." I looked to him for a show of reassurance. He gave none. "I saw a quarrel there once," I ventured.

"Saw? Saw and not heard?"

"No, I heard nothing." I stared blankly ahead. "I saw two people quarrelling, but I heard nothing. Afterwards I wondered if there was really nothing to hear, if they were quarrelling in dumb motion, or if I was insulated in some way."

"Who were the people quarrelling?"

"I didn't recognise them."

"Didn't? Do you mean you couldn't or wouldn't?"

I was silent for a time; it was a difficult question he had posed me. Had I really seen, really heard the quarrel those years ago and closed my eyes and ears because I had not wished to know?"

"Really didn't see, I think," I said finally. "I'm quite short sighted."

"You don't give that impression."

"Now I have contact lenses, then I didn't have."

He accepted that explanation. Indeed, short of actually rapping my eyeball, he could hardly do anything else.

But he acted as though the quarrel, the scene long ago, was important to me now. And I was beginning to see myself that it was crucial.

"Who else was with you when you saw this quarrel?"

"Peter Despenser. He wouldn't remember much; he was a little young even then for his age. Things fade at that age."

"Do they?" he asked dryly. "Who else was there?"

"We were picnicking in the woods. Playing hide and seek. I wasn't so very old myself, and I was lonely. Perhaps the games were a little young for me . . ." My voice died away.

"Who else was there?" he repeated.

"A boy who ran away. Or disappeared. Or was drowned. I've never been quite sure what became of him."

"The Madden boy?"

"You've heard of him? Yes, he was there."

"And shortly afterwards he disappeared?"

"Yes . . . Sometimes I think he didn't go far. Or has come back. And that old Lady Madden knows where he is."

"As to that, I don't know." He was starting the car again.

"Oh, so your investigations haven't included the Maddens?"

He gave me that gentle smile which seemed so strange on the face of a policeman. I was glad he always came alone.

"Yes, they have, as a matter of fact," he said. "I hope I haven't missed out anything or anybody. But I have to weave my way. Not all is clear."

"You are a strange policeman," I said, before I could stop myself. But he wasn't offended, he smiled again and gave a slight shrug.

"You came this way on purpose," I said. "It wasn't my choice at all, really. This is the way you would have driven, whether I wanted or not. You stopped here on purpose, didn't you?"

"I hoped you'd say something," he admitted.

"And have I?"

"Not enough," he said. "Not nearly enough."

He started the car and we drove away, down to the sea, to the little beach where the trees ran nearly down to the sand dunes.

There was a slight breeze and the sky looked blue.

"This was where the boy Madden's clothes were found?"

"Yes. You *do* know all about it."

"I've been digging around."

I wondered if all policemen were like him, anxious to establish the past of their suspects. I had had an idea they were more pragmatic and only sought for evidence that could help them to a conviction.

We sat for a while in silence, and then suddenly I couldn't bear it any more.

"I know I'm deeply under suspicion."

"I can't answer that."

"But you know I have never had any opportunity of buying or in any way getting arsenic?"

"Then that protects you," he said, keeping his eyes on the horizon.

I felt sick, because, although it was true enough that I had had no means of buying arsenic, someone appeared now to have presented me with a little store of it. Certainly there was nothing in the bottle or the packet which had appeared in my home, but who can say what traces might be discovered? Evidence might have been planted on me.

"Tim Alloway is alive and well."

"Then that, too, protects you."

"His wife trusts me."

"How long have you known the Alloways?"

"Only since they moved here."

"You had no meetings with either of them previously?"

"No."

"Did you know that Timothy Alloway has the controlling interest in a metal processing plant, one of whose by-products is white arsenic?"

"No!"

Then he started to question me about the Alloways, although I swore I knew so little. It seemed to me that he wanted to know why they had chosen to rent this summer house and what their relationship was with everybody here.

"Why don't you ask them?" I said in the end.

133

"You sometimes get a better answer by asking other people," he said.

"But why ask me? I know so little. Ask Ben Drummond."

"They've been friends a long time then?"

"I don't know how long. But Ben introduced the Alloways here."

"So he said."

"So you *have* questioned him?"

"You're very protective of Dr. Drummond."

"I don't think so."

"You're obviously fond of him."

I was silent. I was so much more than fond of Ben, so involved, that the words to answer him withered on my lips.

"And he thinks a great deal of you."

"Why did you come and see me so early this morning?"

"Is it early? My working day begins early. I just wanted to talk to you quietly."

"Am I going to be arrested?"

"I hope not."

"That means yes," I cried. "Yes and yes and yes." I could feel my cheek burning like a brand.

He sighed. "I don't think you understand the complexity of the situation."

"You'll never prove I got arsenic through the Alloways, because I didn't."

"It isn't what I shall prove or disprove that you have to worry about, Miss Barclay," he said, starting the car. "Let's get back."

"I don't know why you think I'll believe that," I said bitterly.

He didn't answer as he drove carefully round the curving road from the beach, then he said: "If you want to know, I think you're so emotionally tied up that you can't see the wood for the trees."

I suppose it was his idea of a black joke.

He drove me back to St. John's, and there he asked me the questions he must, all along, have been intending to ask.

"When did your mother die, Miss Barclay?"

"Three years ago."

"And when did you last see her?"

"About eight years before that. I really hardly remember her."

"And when did your father die?"

"Ten years ago. He killed himself after my mother left him. He couldn't bear to live without her. I don't blame him."

"And what happened to you after that, Miss Barclay?"

"I was brought up partly by relations, but truly, mostly by Mrs. Despenser."

"Here?"

"Here. And in Germany and America. They divided me between them for a while. But in the end I came back here. It was what I wished. It was my refuge."

"As it is now?"

I was silent.

"*Where* did your mother die?" he asked then.

"I'm not really sure," I hesitated. "Not quite sure. I think it may have been in Russia. She may have gone from Warsaw to Leningrad and died there. I received the news from the Soviet Embassy. But she *may* have died in Poland."

"She was quite an important person, in her way, wasn't she?"

I cleared my throat. "Well, she belonged to a family which may have been once. In the days when they had princesses and things. But several revolutions have come and gone since then."

"Only one revolution," he said austerely, correcting my loose talk. "She must have loved the country if she went back there to die."

"She didn't know she was going to die. She went there to live."

"She loved it all the more, then."

"She hardly knew it. It was a romantic dream," I cried.

"And you loved your mother?"

I shook my head sadly and silently. "Time took that away."

"I'm not sure I believe that. You strike me as a very loving person."

135

"What is all this about?"

He took a deep breath. I heard the exhalation inside the car. "Do you know I had an anonymous letter telling me you were *a spy*."

"Who am I spying on?" I said. "And where do I do it?" I was trying to sound amused. "I lead a very quiet life here, you know."

"But you travel a good deal," he said, staring at me intently. "Now and in the past you have moved around from country to country. You have no real home."

"That's not true," I said sharply.

"Or perhaps I should say you are at home in several countries. Through you and by means of you, information could be passed."

"And have you a suggestion of any I may have passed?" I said bitterly, feeling that people of mixed parentage are never truly trusted in any society. "Did your anonymous correspondent have any ideas?"

"You once worked in a camp for refugee children in Zürich, which was afterwards found to be a centre of a communications network between Western and Eastern Europe," he said.

I could see in his face that he half believed it; he was well on the way to accepting it as truth. He had weighed me up and decided that this was the sin I was capable of.

How clever he was, my unknown adversary. He had provided for each of us a story we could accept. He had made Ben see me as a Poison Polly, a neurotic poisoner of children; he had made me think of Lynn Alloway as a husband killer, a Florence Maybrick type of murderess; and to this policeman he had suggested treachery, the poisoning of the public wells.

I got out of the car and ran into St. John's.

I was still running as I went up the big staircase. There was no sign of Neil Despenser or Peter, which was just as well. I didn't wish to see either of them just yet. I wanted to get to my room, to pack my things and escape.

But on the way I halted by an open door. Hardly ever during the years I had known St. John's had I seen the doors of the great formal bedroom open. It had been closed since Peter's mother died. Once it had been white and gold, now I could see a flash of melon pink and deep green. I knew it had been redecorated lately and I thought someone had produced a sophisticated colour scheme.

Lily, standing there in her long, green gown, looked out of place. I stood and watched her. She was in front of a looking-glass studying herself. She saw me reflected in the mirror and turned, hand on breast. She smiled, but as usual with her said nothing.

"What are you doing in here, Lily?"

She looked surprised. I imagine surprise was an emotion often felt by Lily; the world must have appeared inexplicable to her on many occasions. What irritated me was how she seemed only to profit by it.

"This is my room," she said. "I've moved in here."

I looked around. She had indeed moved in, her possessions were scattered about. On the bed lay a small suitcase, on the dressing table was a hairbrush and a few pins. A green tweed cloak was folded neatly across the back of a chair. The paucity and even poverty of her belongings touched me in spite of myself. Whether I liked it or not, there was something about Lily that pierced my heart like a thorn.

She moved her hand and I saw it had been covering a pale glitter.

"Where did you get that?" I heard my own voice, high and incredulous.

Since it was an inconvenient question she naturally didn't answer it. "It's huge, isn't it?" she said, with a happy smile.

"Aquamarines have to be huge," I said coldly. "There's no point in them otherwise."

"It's mine now."

She could have taken it from the box in my room. I suppose she had. But it was an ornament which could be worn both as a ring and as a brooch. She was wearing it as a brooch. I didn't think Lily was clever enough to have discovered that for herself, which meant that someone who knew the trick had had to tell her.

"You keep it, Lily," I said. "And enjoy it. Enjoy it while you can."

I left her, closing the door gently and cruelly behind me. That much satisfaction I allowed myself.

In my room I packed my clothes and make-up. I didn't bother to look in the little leather jewel box as I put it away, I could tell by the weight it was empty. I didn't even shed a tear, although I might have done once. I left my suitcase by the door. I would come back for it later. Then I walked down the stairs and out of St. John's.

Outside, I went to the stables and chose a car. I was quite deliberate. They had two cars and a van in St. John's and they could lend me one now. I didn't want to use my own. I wanted a car which might preserve my anonymity for a while, in case I was being followed. For this reason I avoided the big Rover and the glossy Bentley coupé—which was an aristocratic old lady when I was born, and was by now one of the best known cars in the county. I chose the small grey van used for the garden produce (St. John's, like all big houses, sold a lot of its vegetables and fruit) in which I should be virtually invisible. It was parked by the big tank which housed the petrol for the motor grass mower, and the car keys were inside as always.

I drove off. I went as far as my own home and then stopped the van. I could hear music floating out of my house. It was Dvorak's *New World Symphony,* liquid and buoyant, full of hope and courage. I knew it was Mrs. Twining. She couldn't have guessed I would be there to hear, but she put a lot of courage into me with her music. I didn't go in. Instead I drove away.

I had known what I was going to do before I left St. John's, but now I would go out and do it with attack. Attack was the word: I had hitherto been too passive.

But to carry out my plan I must first have an address. Ben would know it but I didn't fancy asking Ben. He would want to know why I needed the address. I could lie, of course, but he would probably be suspicious and might succeed in stopping me doing what I planned to do.

I thought of Lady Madden. She was just the person who might have the knowledge I wanted: She was a great picker-up of odds and ends of knowledge. I could call or

I could use the telephone: I knew she still had a telephone, because I had paid her last bill. I could go back to my own house to telephone, or I could drive down to the road where there was a public telephone box. I chose the latter.

The booth was empty and had its usual smell of stale cigarette smoke and rotten fruit. It was hot in there, and quiet, and a fly buzzed. Beyond me I could see the main road leading to the world outside. Behind me were the woods through which I had come.

I let the phone ring and ring before I left it. I knew she was often slow to answer but answered in the end if she was there: that insatiable curiosity which was embodied in both grandson and grandmother would not let her leave any call unanswered. So she was not at home. Surprising as it may seem, Lady Madden had a wide circle of friends who were delighted to welcome her and nourish her and listen to her gossip and replenish her store.

But before I made another move, I did something I ought to have had the courage to do before. I made a telephone call to the Assistant Director of the Lamb's Hill Remedial Centre. Isobel Bewley was one of my oldest friends, although not a close one.

With a lump in my throat, I said: "Isobel, I gather that some of the sweetmeats I made have caused illness in your children. I'm really very sorry." I was going to say: I am sure my sweetmeats are quite harmless, when, to my surprise, I heard her say:

"It's true we have had a wave of sickness here, but don't blame yourself, my dear. We've had a *plague* of little upsets." She was flustered.

"But do you know what caused them, Isobel?" The edge on my voice got through to her.

"We had to investigate, of course. The theory is that the sweets somehow came into contact with an impurity . . ."

"What sort of impurity?" My voice was hard.

"Arsenic, Anny, but very, very little, just a trace, it *must* have been an accident, and so little, the children were hardly sick at *all*." I suddenly realised that so far
139

from accusing *me* she felt guilty herself, was asking herself whether *she* hadn't, somehow, been to blame.

I didn't feel relief at this realisation. On the contrary, I think it was at that moment I grasped how easy it was to manipulate people and their emotions. I felt as if the ground was moving beneath my feet.

"Why has nothing been said to me directly?" I asked.

"Not all the children who ate your sweets were ill, it didn't seem clear—nothing is clear." Her voice trailed away. Poor unhappy Isobel.

"And about the child that died," I began.

"Ah, there, I can reassure you." Her voice grew stronger. "The post mortem showed the cause clearly: the heart was only half the size it should have been. And there were other abnormalities we hadn't suspected. The poor little thing could have died at any time."

I suppose we exchanged a few more words, but I didn't take them in. Instead I heard the fly buzzing and buzzing.

I stood there and let the fly move up and down the window in front of me while I thought. The fly disappeared, and a name came into my mind: Nurse Knolly. She was so close to Dr. Ben Drummond that she would know who had started the rumour that the child died of arsenic.

She answered the telephone at once. It was one of her gifts always to be at the end of the telephone when it rang; a great gift for a nurse.

"Hello."

"Anna Barclay."

"Oh, yes." She sounded surprised. "I thought you were ill."

"Who told you that?"

"Dr. Ben."

"I'm not ill. Upset, perhaps, but not ill."

She coughed. "I'm sure you're under strain." She didn't sound unsympathetic. She was a little jealous of me, because of Ben's interest in me, but I was under his protection.

"Will you help me?" I didn't wait for her to answer this

140

question, but went on. "There is a lot of gossip, malicious stories, being spread about me."

There was a pause, then she said, "I believe I have heard something."

"I think there must be one common source for them. One person must have started it. You get about a lot, do you know who it can be?"

If Ben knew a name then she knew, and if she knew one then Ben knew it. That was how it worked with them. And I badly wanted to learn exactly what Ben knew.

I waited. I could almost hear her totting up in her mind whether Ben would want me to know anything. Finally she came down on the side of caution. "Well, I'm not sure," she said.

"Please try," I said.

"You know, my memory's so bad," she said. I knew she had a memory like a tape recorder.

"No," she said finally. "I can't seem to pin anything down. Of course, I *have* heard some stories, bu I didn't pay much attention."

"Can't you even remember who spoke to you?" I said.

"No," she said blandly.

Liar, I thought. I put the receiver down before she could speak again.

As I turned into the main road I was glad I had come in the van. I saw Ben's car racing towards me and on towards the road from which I had just emerged. Hunched over his wheel, he never gave me a glance.

I would have been angrier with Nurse Knolly if I had not remembered I knew a woman who made a habit of being well informed.

She was about fifteen years older than me, plumpish and with orange red hair. I used to think that her orange lipstick matched her hair and I never knew which was the more artificial. Emigrating from a big city advertising bureau, she had built herself a local business. She had come to me seeking recipes for a new sort of cooking chocolate she was helping test-market in this area. My recipes had been successful and Tessa Mann thought I had scored. She got a new account and I got a debt of gratitude. I thought my time had come to cash this debt.

It would mean an extra hour's drive to her office in our county town but I undertook it willingly. I felt as anonymous as a bird as I sped down the motorway. It was the first time in days I had been off the peninsula. It was a good feeling.

Tessa was in her office when I went in, bandying words with her new young assistant, a good-looking lad of about my own age. Her assistants, built on much the same lines, came and went frequently. I never thought there was much doubt about her interest in them. Or how they got on. Three months of Tessa and they must have been heading for freedom and Men's Lib.

"Nice to see you," said Tessa. She always said that, she might, indeed, have meant it, although I didn't rely on it. "I'm thinking of using you again on recipes."

"Not beginning with an A, I hope."

"No, for onions," she said seriously. I was glad she wasn't joining in jokes about arsenic. "Stagger off now, boy," she said to her assistant. "I'll see you later." She gave him a hearty slap.

"You'll kill him," I said.

"Not him. He loves it."

"I'll be glad to help you over onions, but meanwhile can you help me?"

She looked hopeful; I wondered what she thought I wanted. I felt almost apologetic, as if I was disappointing her, when all I said was simply, "Tessa, someone's spreading gossip about me and I want the name. Can you get it?"

She looked at me, licking her orange lipstick as if it tasted good.

"Oh, come on, Tess," I said. "If you know anything tell me now."

"No, I don't know anything. I'm a good guesser, though, when it comes to sex and trouble."

"I never said it was sex."

"Bound to be, dear. Somewhere." This was her profound conviction. "And if it is, then look for someone close to you."

"Is that what you call good guessing?"

"It's worked with me in the past," she said equably.

"When I got my second divorce I received a whole stream of poisonous letters. And who wrote them? My own dear husband. So look around, dear, look around." She watched me. "Maybe you know more than you think."

I knew where I must go next. I knew it without conscious thought; it seemed the inevitable step to take. I had this feeling that I had been groping around long enough. I wanted to get on solid ground at last.

So I went to the police. I knew where the building was placed in the county town, because I had once been there at the time when Robert Madden disappeared. The big, square building looked, and even smelt the same. I have heard that it is sounds you remember and not sights; but I think that smells are the great memory-makers. The scents of dust and disinfectant that hung around this place took me back once again to the time when the boy went. I had to swallow hard and tell myself that I was a grown woman and no longer a frightened girl.

A uniformed policeman sat staring at me with sceptical indifference from behind a desk. Even his desk had a barrier in front of it, he was doubly fenced in. No doubt it was the best way. After all, one doesn't want to be *welcomed* to a police station. If he had come forward with an outstretched hand I would probably have recoiled. It *ought* to be a struggle to be heard by the forces of law and order, that way one knows the universal rules still hold and the world still swings on its old axis of concern and apathy.

"Well, miss?" he said, after waiting for me to speak.

"I want to speak to Inspector Dilke." I didn't know his rank, if he had told me then I'd forgotten, but Inspector sounded about right.

"Eh?"

"I'm not sure if he is an Inspector or has a higher rank but his name is James Dilke," I explained; I could hear my voice shaking.

"I see."

"I'd like to speak to him." He still seemed resistant to the idea.

"We haven't got him here."

143

"But you could tell me how to find him."

"No."

"Oh, come on, *please*," I said.

He shook his head slowly and pressed a bell. "Maybe you'd better have a word with someone else. I don't seem able to convince you."

I was outside again within ten minutes. And with me I took the knowledge that there was not, and never had been, a Detective Inspector James Dilke.

10

I was completely at a loss. What had seemed known, apprehended fact had vanished into thin air. I had been living in a nightmare. I drove back to the woods and St. John's almost without thinking about it. I was there before I realised I had had a choice. Or did I truly have one? Wasn't there something that bound me to St. John's?

On the most practical level of all there was, of course, the van. I didn't plan to steal it. Perhaps I had deliberately chosen their car so I would have to come back. I wouldn't put it past me at all. I was beginning to see I was that sort of girl. I parked the van in the garage, where it was as if it had never been away. A larger van was already there, complete with ladders and tins of paint, so I knew the decorators had arrived.

I went in through the back of the house, through the big arched rooms which had once been the original kitchen and were now used only as storerooms. A more modern pantry lay beyond. Here Mrs. Mac was stirring something in a saucepan. She looked up when she saw me.

"Hello, Miss Barclay." I could see she had decided on her tone with me: she was going to be friendly but not warm. Between me and Lily she was having a difficult time. I looked round to see if Lily was there but she wasn't. I supposed she was out tending her seeds, wearing

145

a valuable aquamarine and a William Morris style gown.

"I'm afraid you've missed lunch," she said, with the air of one who's not going to do anything about it. "This is dinner I'm engaged with now."

"I'm not hungry."

She continued to stir. I could see she was making a plain white sauce and I could smell that she hadn't put in enough bouquet garni; you really ought to infuse it in the milk you use for the sauce to get the right flavour. Mrs. Mac produced good food of a simple sort, but I wouldn't say much for the sensitivity of her taste buds. It suggested that her erstwhile august employers had liked their food to be of a somewhat bland sort.

"You ought to eat. You need strength." She gave the sauce a final flurry of stirs. "You had another visitor while you were out."

"Oh?"

"A fat old woman came looking for you."

Lady Madden, I thought, instantly alert.

"Anything else to add?" I said. "I mean to fill out the picture."

"Social class doubtful," said Mrs. Mac. "Her habits not in the least doubt. She smelt strongly of cheap port."

"Oh dear." This was bad news. It meant she hadn't managed to cadge the money for gin or whisky and was drinking British Medicinal Port. "You're sure it was port? Not gin or whisky?"

"I hope I know the difference between wine and spirits," said Mrs. Mac primly. "It was port. And not vintage port, either."

Gin made Lady Maddin gay, but port unbalanced her. Whisky was her best drink, really; it seemed to steady her.

"So she came here, and you thought she was drunk and she went away again. Didn't she say anything? Leave a message?"

"She walked in while I was cleaning the cooker. Seemed to know her way around. I said you were out. Then some- one called her name from the garden and she went out."

"Who called her?"

She turned away. "The boy, I think."

"I'll talk to Peter." I moved towards the door.

"If you can find him."

"What do you mean?"

She shrugged. "He wasn't in to lunch."

"Who was then?"

"His father. And I had the company of My Lady Lily."

I knew then where she had placed Lily: as someone who would never be received at court.

"Are they still in?"

"Lily went out after lunch, with one of the young painters working on the house, to show him the young seedlings she was bringing on. Heartsease, she said they were called." Mrs. Mac's voice was a miracle of detachment.

"Violets is another name," I said. "And Mr. Neil, is he in?"

"I dare say."

"Well, thanks for telling me about Lady Madden. I'm sorry I've missed her, when she came all this way to see me."

"Oh, so that's her name, is it? Well, the Queen never gave her that title."

"I think she did, in fact. Or her grandfather did." I was amused. "Sir James Madden was British Minister in Tokyo or Peking or somewhere like that years and years ago. He married Lady Madden when she was only nineteen."

"Romantic," said Mrs. Mac, with a sceptical sniff.

"Yes, I think it must have been," I said, seeing the Peking of years ago. The Maddens had lived in a Chinese palace with paper windows oiled to admit the light, and St. John and his lady had dined in a tree-lined courtyard, the warm air scented with lotus. The Chinese servants in their blue cotton coats and red satin waistcoats had carried the dishes from under the curved roofs and through the lacquered columns to where a white-haired old gentleman and a young girl sat in full evening dress at a candle-lit table set with fine linen and glass and silver. Yes, it must have been romantic. To think about it was like stirring a pot of pot-pourri.

I left the kitchen and took my stealthy way up the back staircase so that I could get my case without being seen and escape to my own house. I hoped to avoid seeing anyone.

I had reached the great hall, with my case in one hand and Jackson's cage in the other, when I saw that the library door was open. Today there was no music playing and for a moment I thought that no one was there. Then I saw Neil Despenser was sitting at the blue and gold cloisonné writing table. His head was turned away and he didn't see me. For a moment I watched him. When people are unobserved they often reveal a side you hadn't seen before. As I saw him now, he appeared both tired and unhappy. He looked up and saw me then.

"Hello, Anna." I saw his eyes flick over my case, but he said nothing. I put my case down as unobtrusively as I could and placed Jackson, who was either dead or asleep, beside it. Then I went into the room.

"What's the matter with you?"

"It's Peter. He's done a bunk."

"Is that what you call it?"

He sighed. "I suppose it's an unkind way of putting it."

"It's not a very fatherly way of putting it," I said slowly.

"Sometimes I don't feel like a father to Peter, and he feels it too. He acts as if he was a changeling. Haven't you noticed it?"

"I'd noticed something. I'm not sure if it's what you think it is, though. I'm sure he feels he's your son. What makes you think he's run away?"

"He's not around, is he?"

"He's a boy of sixteen. He might just have gone for a long walk in the woods to look at the birds."

"He wouldn't stay out so long without a reason," said Neil obstinately. "I watch him. I know the pattern of the way he lives. This is out of the pattern."

"You don't trust him, do you? He must love that."

"I'm sitting here waiting. If he comes back, I won't say a thing."

"And what do you think he's running from?" I asked.

"I wish to God I knew," said Neil Despenser.

"I think he's running away from *you*," I said, turning back to pick up my case and the patient Jackson.

I got as far as the door.

He gripped my arm and jerked me to a halt. "And what does that mean?"

"Peter has been frightened of someone ever since you got back. Perhaps even before. That's obvious. Who else is there but you?"

"There's you."

"Oh yes, I think Peter is a little frightened of me. It's understandable. I think he has reason to be frightened. He has a guilty conscience. He's done one or two things against me."

"Tell me what."

And then, when I hesitated—"Come, Anna, I have a right to know."

"I think he started the fire in my house, and also left a packet labelled poison in my hat box. Just tricks."

"And now you think he's frightened I will discover what he's done?"

"He may feel he has disappointed you."

"That's an ambiguous remark."

"Well, he wasn't doing what he did to me just for fun. Who was he trying to please?"

"Do you think *I* want to harm you? So that's it, is it?"

I was quiet for a moment. Down below I could hear Mrs. Mac bang a door hard. I could even hear the distant sound of the painters' voices.

"He might have thought you wanted that. Or at the very least perhaps he thought you wanted me frightened."

"Anny, what sort of a man do you think I am?"

"I think you're a liar and a cheat and a bit of a sadist," I said.

When he was angry, the colour of his eyes seemed to change, and became darker and brighter, the iris itself becoming black.

"Well, that does seem to be the end of the day," he said.

To my shame, I found that I was crying freely. Tears rolled out of my eyes and splashed, warm as blood, on my hand. I wiped them away, wretchedly.

"I think I must tell you what I have discovered," I began, my mind full of policemen who were not policemen and multiple poisonings which had never taken place. But some facts stood out hard and clear and could not

149

be denied. It was established that Tim Alloway had taken arsenic: I had Ben's word for that as true. It was established that Neil Despenser knew the pseudo-policeman James Dilke: I had Mrs. Mac as a witness to that as a fact. "Well, to begin with I knew the stories about me handing out poison are malicious nonsense, a fiction invented to destroy me or something about me."

"My dear Anna," Neil started to say.

"And I know James Dilke, whom you also know, is not a policeman."

He stared at me. "My dear, ridiculous, unhappy girl!"

"That's not good enough," I said fiercely. "I'm not a child in the nursery, crying because I've fallen and grazed my knees."

"Falling flat on your face is exactly what I'm trying to stop you doing, Anny," he said.

I knew I ought to cover my ears and not listen; he could always persuade. There was something hypnotic to me in the tones of that voice, in the shape of those eyes. I could sense the curve of the eyeball in the socket, the nerves behind the iris, the brain behind the nerves, the imagination that drove it all. If I listened I should be mastered.

"Let's leave it," I said. "I've been foolish, even demanding, I suppose, without meaning to be. But I see that my very existence is a demand. I was foolish not to recognise that."

"Oh, Anny!"

I could try to close my eyes, my ears, but I couldn't inhibit my feelings. I couldn't control my skin, or my muscles, or my blood vessels. When he put his hand on mine, I enjoyed the touch, and my body showed it. I'd let myself down, as usual. It was no good drawing away. The damage was done, and to both of us.

Only he, of course, was never truly at a loss. Perhaps he might appear so, hesitate now and then, look tender, or seem doubtful of what to do next, but even while it affected me I marked it down as pretence.

"Anny, silly silly Anny."

Wise old Anny, suspicious old Anny, and silly innocent

young Anny at the same time, they were rolled up together and one of them was struggling to get out.

"I'd like to think you trust me, but, anyway, you might listen to me. Now, keep quiet, you silly girl."

How could I speak with his arms round me and my face pressed against him? I hardly even wanted to speak. It was lovely to be reassured. "I want to believe you," I murmured.

"I should think so, indeed." He held me away. "No, Anna, I'm going down to the cellar and I'm getting out that champagne I promised you and we'll have some now. Then we'll talk."

"No champagne."

"Yes. It'll give me strength to talk to you. And I have to talk," he said, his voice serious. "Wait here a minute. No, I'm afraid to leave you alone. You and Peter . . . You're sure you don't know anything about that?"

We were half-way down the cellar stairs when we met a young painter running up. He looked both excited and frightened at the same time. He was in such a hurry that he was past us before he stopped. He turned and spun back. "Sir," he said. "Sir."

"Where are you off to?" said Neil.

"I'm going for the police," said the boy. Then he gave a gasp and sat down suddenly on a stair, his face white. "Maybe you'd better do it," he said, his voice thick. "I don't feel too good."

In the low vaults which were the cellars, and the oldest part of the house, another painter was crouching round a square of earth on the floor. He looked up as we came in.

"It's under this flagstone," he said in an excited voice. "We were larking about see, me and my mate, and we saw this flagstone was loose and Ron said, 'Let's have it up in case they've got a body buried underneath.' " He gave Neil a half horrified, half fascinated look as he did so.

Neil went over and stared down at the exposed brown earth under the paving stone. Slowly I moved behind him to look down in my turn.

151

I could see a small brown clawlike object protruding from the dry soil.

"Go upstairs, Anna," said Neil in a stern, cold voice. "And stay there till I come." He tried to move between me and the object of my gaze.

"Looks like a monkey, don't it?" whispered the lad raptly.

I stared in horror. In spite of what the boy had said what I could see was unmistakably human even if withered and shrunk. There was a hand, an arm, a skull. Even recognition was not beyond me. There was a bush, unkempt and loose, of dusty red hair. I knew then I was looking at Robert Madden, not lost, not drowned, but buried here, waiting to be found.

Upstairs, hardly knowing how I had got there, I didn't pause. I took up Jackson's cage and my case. I still had my own car in the old stables. I got in and drove away from St. John's and out into Ironwood.

I was in my kitchen, whipping up a dish of taramasalata, which, in case you don't know, is made up of smoked cod's roe, olive oil, bread and lemon juice. I was making some to deep-freeze as an experiment; I didn't fancy eating it at the moment; I didn't fancy eating anything; I doubted if I would ever eat happily again. Meanwhile, I went on mixing the cod's roe and the olive oil. It was beginning to look palatable. A summer ago I had included a recipe for taramasalata in a cookery course I gave, and for weeks afterwards, wherever you dined out on the peninsula, you were always offered taramasalata.

The advantage of taramasalata is that you can cook it all without the use of electricity and I still had no power in my kitchen. I was cooking, not for hunger nor for love, but as therapy. I hoped it would stop me thinking.

As I stood there, looking out of the window, the trees seemed very near. I had never realised before how enclosed by them my home was. It was a house hidden in the woods. Outside the trees were dark and heavy with their summer leafage. The air felt oppressive and hot. I thought there might be a storm coming. I opened the window, and listened to the leaves moving in the wind.

I knew I should have the police here soon and perhaps that was the storm I was dreading. They would be asking me what I remembered about the Madden boy and the day he disappeared. I could say I remembered nothing and perhaps they might believe me. Probably not, though. James Dilke had hardly believed me. I had to remind myself however that he was not a policeman. It was strange that, even now, I could hardly believe it.

I had just put the taramasalata in a dish into the freezer when I heard a key in the front door.

Mrs. Twining walked into the kitchen. She looked tired and untidy.

"I saw your light on, so I came on in."

"I'm cooking."

"So I see. Decided to come back then?"

"Yes." I didn't feel the need to amplify with Mrs. Twining. She'd fill in the story her own way in any case. And in due course she'd hear the truth. Or as much of the truth as ever became clear. "Thanks for coming in. I'm fine, though."

"I'm glad about that." She was fiddling with the cooking utensils on the table. She started to wash up a spoon and fork I had been using. "Of course, I didn't really just happen to be passing. I came round on purpose."

"I'd guessed." You couldn't pass my house on your way from A to B. It wasn't near anywhere, except Ben's place. If you came here it was because you meant to come. "How did you know I was here?"

"I didn't know you were here. How could I? I haven't got extrasensory perception. Often wished I had." She sounded wistful. "Mind you, I've tried, but there's nothing in it for me. No, I've been coming round every night to check up."

"That's good of you," I said, surprised. Interesting and hard-working as she was, Mrs. Twining usually didn't do a thing if she wasn't paid for it.

"Oh well, I'll put in my little bill," she said. "But I wanted to keep an eye on things. That was a nasty little fire you had. You could have been killed."

I nodded. "That's what I thought."

"I don't think it was natural, that fire. I know we all have accidents, but that wasn't one. Even before the fire

154

I got the feeling there was someone *watching* your house. Hanging about, you know."

"Not *still?*" I said uneasily.

"Might be my imagination." She had cleared the table efficiently. "Before you had the fire I thought there might have been someone in the house when we weren't there."

"You didn't tell me."

"I'm telling you now. In a rather flighty mood you've been lately." She looked at me sideways. "Coming, going. Getting a rose every day. I thought you had something on your mind."

"What *did* happen?"

"The night you were out cooking at Mrs. Alloway's I came in to tidy up. I thought there was someone here. It had that feel. Then the door closed. I swear it did. It's never been secure, that door. I ran to the door and called. Silly, really."

"Did you see anyone?"

"No. I thought perhaps it was the doctor. He's always in and out, isn't he? But still I was nervous. I took to wedging the door. And then the next day you had the fire."

"The next day I had the fire," I agreed. It was strange how events were working themselves out. Now I knew that Mrs. Twining had wedged the back door from the inside. But she had certainly not laid the fire which burned my kitchen.

So perhaps the person who had started the fire had meant only to frighten me and not to kill me. It was only a hope, really. I was beginning to feel a new kind of terror: the threats which had hung over me seemed to be changing shape as I approached them. I was walking forward into a mist in which phantoms continually formed and then dispersed.

"I felt better when you were up at St. John's, really," said Mrs. Twining, breaking into my thoughts. "I don't like you being all alone here." She buttoned her coat, preparatory to going. "I mean, here you are alone in the woods like Little Red Riding Hood."

Cinderella, Little Red Riding Hood, Bluebeard, all the childhood stories are terrifying if we think about them. At the heart of every nursery tale lie mystery and fear.

Nor do they lose their powers as we grow up. On the contrary, childhood phantoms often walk on adult streets and come into our homes and live with us.

Ironwood and St. John's, what story was this? Was it the story of the Sleeping Beauty? Was I the Sleeper and what was I seeing now I awoke? Not my lover awakening me with a kiss. I gave an involuntary shudder.

"Don't go near St. John's, Mrs. Twining," I said. "Stay away. That's my advice. Stay away."

I was alone and at home and it was forever. Sleeping Beauty had woken up and had found the Prince's face terrifying.

The telephone rang and I let it ring, but I knew it was no good. In the end the world would get in. The telephone call was probably from the police, this time the real police. Already they must know I had been at St. John's and had left. They would wish to question me. Any minute now there could be a knock on the door and a detective would be asking me if I was Anna Barclay.

Before the telephone rang again I made a call myself to Lady Madden's house. The telephone rang but there was no answer. I could imagine it ringing through an empty house. It must be empty. I knew if she was there Lady Madden would answer a caller. Drunk or sober, she loved her telephone, it made her feel important.

I made myself some coffee and drank it slowly. Then I tried again. Still no answer.

I smoked a cigarette and watched the clock crawl round for fifteen minutes before once more I dialled Lady Madden's number. She didn't answer.

The conclusion was inescapable; she was not there. I was alone in the woods and my only ally, God help me, was out. Or drunk.

Then I heard a motor car arrive. Jackson started to mutter. There came a couple of short brisk raps on the door. The door shook a little.

"Hello, Ben."

"I'd have knocked the door in if you hadn't opened."

"I know it."

He came into the kitchen and stood looking at me

young and cross and tired. But there was an element of triumph in the flower pinned to his buttonhole. Perhaps at last it was his flower and not an imitation of his father's.

"I've been trying to ring you."

"Oh, it was you," I said thoughtlessly.

"So you *were* in." He looked round the room.

"There's no one else here," I said.

"Why did you come back here alone?"

"I had a quarrel with Neil Despenser," I said, after a moment's thought.

"Did you? He didn't tell me."

"He doesn't tell you everything."

"He told me you'd gone, though."

"What else did he tell you?"

"Not that you'd come here." It seemed to rankle.

"I don't suppose he knew." I couldn't keep the feeling out of my voice.

"You hate him, don't you?" said Ben. "Temporarily, no doubt. That's the way of it with you and him."

"You think so?"

"Oh yes. You're for him, then against him. I don't know what he does to you."

"Nothing, absolutely nothing."

He gave a short laugh. "And I never know which you enjoy more. The times you hate him or the times you love him."

"No more loving." I shook my head.

"I wish I could believe that, Anny."

"I couldn't forget him. We must move away from here. But, once I'm away from Ironwood and St. John's, I believe I'll be free," I said steadily.

"We could emigrate," said Ben. He gripped my hand. "I've wanted to go for a long time. Would you really come?"

"Yes, oh yes."

"We'd leave everything behind." He put his arms around me and rested his head on my hair. I could feel his protective, possessive pressure all round me. For a moment I gave myself up to feeling safe and secure. "But it would have to be soon, Anny."

157

"There'd be things to arrange," I said, still relaxed against him.

"Oh sure." I could hear his easy breathing. "But nothing important, together we can do anything."

"Quite important," I said with a sigh, drawing away. "For instance, up at St. John's the body of Robert Madden has been found. He was buried in the cellar."

"Robert Madden! I can't believe it."

"It's true, though. I didn't want to tell you. He must have been buried there by Peter or his father. Or perhaps by both."

"I never believed he'd be found." His face was quite white. "I must go up there."

"No, please don't go. You can't do a thing."

But his face was stern. "We can't run away from it, my darling. I can't not any longer. I must find out for sure what is going on up there."

"Let me come then." I felt I couldn't bear to let him go alone. I held his arm.

"No." He put me gently aside. "This I do on my own." At the door he stopped and kissed me.

"Lock the door behind me and don't open it. Don't talk to anyone and don't let anyone in till I get back. Promise me?"

"I promise." I closed the door behind him and let him go.

I suppose I should have kept my promise if the voice that called me had been any other voice.

When I did not answer the first knock on the door I could hear him calling, softly at first and then louder.

"Anny, Anny."

I stood behind the door, listening, but not answering.

"Anny, I know you're there. I can *see* you, silly Anny."

There was a tiny slit for letters high up on the solid door. He must have had his eyes pressed to it.

"Peter," I said, and, in defiance of everything Ben had said, I opened the door.

"Oh, Anny." He leaned towards me, as if weak. I reached out my hand and steadied him. "Why did you pretend you weren't there?"

"I didn't."

"I could *feel* you pretending. You were trying to disappear." He closed his eyes.

"You'd better come in and sit down," I said, not in too friendly a voice, either.

"No, I'm all right. Anyway, we must get going."

"I'm not going anywhere."

"It's Lady Madden, Anny." He paused, aware perhaps (and with that family who could say what they calculated on?) that he had said the one name that could move me. "You must come to her."

He must have seen the look of suspicion on my face. "Don't look at me like that, Anny, as if I'd done wrong. Don't you know I've had enough of that?"

"Yes, I know."

"That's why I'm on my way. I heard Lady Madden was asking for you at the house and I met her in the garden. She saw that I wanted to get out and she said you come with me and I'll give you the wherewithal. I didn't have any money. Would you have given me any? No, never mind, it doesn't matter."

"She hasn't got any money herself."

"But she went to get it. She said you'll be the second boy to go, and I know where to get you some money."

"I suppose she wants her little bit of revenge," I said slowly. "And she certainly knows how to get it." I had to remember that Lady Madden could not yet know her grandson's body had been found, but certainly she would know that his son's flight would cut Neil Despenser into two parts.

"She said wait for me in the woods. In Ironwood, you know, where the old furnaces were."

"I know. And I suppose she never came?"

"No. So I went to her house. She's ill, Anny."

"Drunk," I said.

"*No*. She's on the floor. And she said, tell Anny to get the doctor."

I looked at him steadily. "Are you telling the truth, Peter?"

He flushed, and then went white. I suppose for most of

his adolescence all of us had been putting that question to him in one way and another.

"All right" I said, suddenly. "I believe you. I'll get the car out."

"Peter," I said. "Is that blood on your hand?" There was a dried red streak across the palm of his right hand and continuing upwards to make a small stain on his cuff.

"I don't know," he said, and looked young and frightened. I could feel my own heart thudding.

We went into Lady Madden's little house. As always entry was easy. She rarely locked her doors. "Nothing to steal, dear," she used to say.

"Is this how you got in, Peter?"

"Yes." He nodded.

"Where is she?"

"In her sitting-room." He pointed to the open door.

She was lying back on the sofa, eyes closed, as if she had sunk back when suddenly feeling tired. On a table beside her were a bottle and an empty glass.

"Stay at the door, Peter," I ordered. Then I went up to her and took her hand. It was flaccid. Across the back was a long angry scratch. I bent forward and looked into her face, which was empty of expression.

"She's dead, isn't she?" asked Peter from the door.

"Yes." I laid her hands together in her lap and stepped back. "I suppose it was always on the cards. Probably she's had a stroke. But there's blood on her hair. And here, on her hand. Did you touch her?"

"I might have done."

"That's where you got the blood on you."

"She must have been dying when she spoke to me."

"Yes." I could see that he was trembling slightly. "I think we had better do what she asked and get the doctor. I know where he is. It means going up to the house."

"St. John's?"

"St. John's," I said. I closed the door behind me quietly, as if it mattered any more.

As we set off, I said to Peter, "You know, in the last few hours both you and I have run away from St. John's,

160

and now we are both going back. There must be a joke there, if we could only see it."

We drove into St. John's by the back road, a long bumpy drive which led to the old stables.

"Why are we coming this way?" said Peter, uneasily.

I knew I had to start talking to him. "What was the house like when you left? All quiet?"

"We had workmen in," he said, still uneasy. "Why?"

"I came in later than you, after you'd gone. The workmen made a discovery in the cellar."

He didn't say anything but waited, silent. I kept my eyes straight on the road. "It was the body of Robert Madden, I think."

"Robert?" There was unmistakable relief in his voice. "Then everyone will know it had nothing to do with me, which is what you all thought, isn't it? I didn't kill him, I didn't bury him." There was a sob in his voice. "Isn't it funny how things turn out? I don't mind going back now. I can face anything."

I drove on. My own feelings were less straightforward. All those years ago, when the Madden boy had died, Peter had been almost a child. He hadn't buried a body under the flagstones of St. John's. But someone had buried it, and it wasn't a stranger. "Good," I said. "We'll face it together."

"Don't run away from Dad," said Peter.

"I have done," I said. "C'est fini." It was a relief to have said it.

"You were marvellous to me in Paris."

"I was a bit. I enjoyed it, though." I suppose I was saying goodbye to him with these words. The boy Peter I had babied in Paris would not be around any more. "I was marvellous to myself, too."

"Lovely old Anny," he said, reaching out and touching my arm gently. "I don't know why you're not married. To someone attractive and nice like yourself."

"I was in love once," I said dreamily.

"Was he madly attractive?"

"I thought so."

"As well as attractive, was he nice?"

"Yes, in some ways, very nice."

161

"Why did you leave him?"

"I don't usually tell people this, but, as a matter of fact, he left me."

"Oh, Anny." He sounded sorry and sad. "What a shame."

"He was selfish, bone idle, and used to having always his own way."

"I thought you said he was *nice*?"

"You can be all those things and nice as well, unfortunately."

Everything was still and sweet in the green tunnel the trees formed above us, but I had never been more tense and on the alert.

"I suppose there'll be policemen, Anny?"

"Oh yes, there'll be policemen," I said. I slid the car over the old cobbles and under the arch which led to the stables.

We got out of the car. I was thinking rapidly about the best way of getting hold of Ben without attracting attention I didn't want, when I saw a girl come through the arch. It was Lily.

She was the last person I either wished or expected to see. Unpredictable as ever, she gave me a brilliant smile. She was no longer wearing my aquamarine.

"I *am* glad to see you."

"What are you doing round here, Lily?"

"Why, I'm looking for my husband." She looked very beautiful as she said the words. There was a sort of gloss on her, which both touched and saddened me.

"He *can't* be your husband," I said wearily.

"Oh yes." She raised her head with dignity.

"How long have you been married, Lily?" I asked.

"Years." She smiled. "Years."

"If true, it makes some things a good deal easier," I said.

We were standing by the petrol pump and I saw that someone had let quite a puddle of petrol drip from the pipe.

"Shall I move the car farther in," said Peter, in a muffled voice. He had his head turned away, as if he didn't want to meet Lily.

"No, don't bother," I said sharply. It was too late for him to go hiding his head; there were certain things he had to face.

I heard Lily give a little cry and turned round to see her facing a tall figure.

"Oh, Ben," I said, "I'm glad you're here."

"Come out of the car, Peter," said Ben. "I can see you."

Peter finished reparking the car and came forward. "Hello, Ben," he said.

"I thought I told you not to come here," said Ben to me. He was breathing hard, as if he'd been hurrying.

"We were looking for you."

"What, all of you?" said Ben, glancing around.

"Yes," said Lily.

Yes is such a little word, but this one was big and heavy enough to change my whole life.

I looked at Ben and saw there the reflection of Lily's word.

Ben and I were bonded together by so many ties, our youth together, the old friendship between our fathers, and, in the end, by the scar on my face. And yet, I had a sudden, vivid picture of Ben and Lily, meeting in one of the secluded rooms in St. John's, lying together on one of the great old four poster beds. I could picture them in a clandestine meeting in the semi-deserted house to which Ben always had an entrance. Like me, he knew many ways in. And I knew then with a complete return of memory that Ben and Lily had been the quarrelling pair I had seen so long ago. My mind had deliberately blurred the details so that I could forget.

"Oh Ben," I said. "Are you married to Lily?"

"Of course I'm not married to her."

"You are," cried Lily. "You are, you are, you are."

"She thinks so," I said. "And you could be."

"No," said Ben.

"Did Robert see you together? Were you seen by him in St. John's? Perhaps he followed you."

"I could never be married to a girl like Lily," said Ben. "You can see that for yourself." His voice was hard. Robert Madden wouldn't have stood much chance against that determination. Some time he had followed Ben to

163

St. John's, or been lured there, and died there for his pains, and been buried where he died. Then his clothes had been placed by the sea to point to a different kind of death.

"We're wed," cried Lily.

"I can see she wouldn't be a wife for a rising young doctor," I said.

"I love *you*," said Ben.

"And besides, I'm richer," I continued.

"You're going to take some convincing, I can see," he said angrily.

"Peter," I called. "Come over here and admit that you played the trick about POISON FOR CATS on me?"

"I'm sorry, Anny," he whispered. "I have black moods. I *did* want to hurt you. Not the fire, though. Only the silly note about cats."

"You know, I understand that about you, and even think I've earned it." I said, keeping my voice steady. "But who suggested it?"

Peter's eyes moved to Ben, but he did not answer.

"Admit that you've been in continuous touch with Ben all the while you've been away?"

"We've kept up," mumbled Peter.

"You've only his word," said Ben. "My God, how can you do this to me?"

The smoke curled up from Ben's cigarette, past the flower pinned in his lapel. I looked at the pin and remembered the scratch on Lady Madden's hand. "I believe you killed them both," I said. "Lady Madden and her grandson." I looked at Lily, but no help was forthcoming there. Peter was a doubtful quantity. Any more pressure on him and I thought he would go to pieces. But in myself I felt new strength.

"You've terrorised the boy. Just as you made him your victim over Robert Madden's disappearance. And what was Robert blackmailing you over? Lily? Or something else?"

Lily started to sob. "Why are you shouting at my husband?"

"Don't cry, Lily," I said wearily. I couldn't take the sight of her tears. "He isn't worth your tears."

"But my baby was," said Lily. "I cry for my baby. I remember now that I am crying for him."

I stared at her, deeply shocked by her words.

"They told me in the hospital in Geneva that this was why I cried," said Lily, with simple dignity. "And I must believe them because at first I cried without stopping."

"I didn't know you'd had a baby, Lily," I whispered.

"Of course, there was no baby," said Ben.

"A little, little baby two inches long from tail to head," said Lily. "But it never swam like a fish in the world." Her lips curved in a Madonna smile.

"My God," I said. I felt sick as I saw so clearly what had happened to Lily and what part Ben had played in her history. I turned to face him.

"*No*," he said.

"Now I know what you had to suppress at any price," I said. "And the price was Robert Madden's life and Lily's sanity. Yes, and I suppose we can add Lady Madden to that list. Once Lily met her grandmother again then nothing would have kept Lady Madden from getting all the details from Lily. Then she would know you were a killer."

I think I was shouting because when I stopped talking a silence seemed to fall.

"I'm going into the house," I said, suddenly seeing St. John's as salvation. "I want to see Neil."

"Take it steady," said Ben. He moved away from Lily, who stood there looking wretched. "You don't think I'm letting you up into that madhouse, police, everyone milling about?" He took a cigarette out of his pocket and lit it. "Relax and calm down, my dear girl. I'm beginning to think all these stories floating around have unsteadied your mind."

"If they *are* floating around, then you are their source," I said. "You and your assistant, Nurse Knolly."

He shook his head. "In your way, you're as bad as Lily. What a monstrous thing to say."

"Yes, you wanted me to seem a monster, even to think myself one. Anything to keep me from Neil." Earlier, I had thought: I am going to be killed, murdered. In a way I had been right, but I saw now that my death was to have been spiritual and emotional rather than physical.

165

I was, simply, to have been absorbed as a wealthy property of Ben's, useful to him to promote his future career. I turned round. "Peter, get up to the house."

"Don't do that, Peter," said Ben, not looking at the boy. Peter stood irresolute, moving from foot to foot. Nothing could have demonstrated Ben's power over him more strongly.

"Leave the boy alone," I said, my voice shaking. "Leave him *alone*. He's had enough. From us all."

"I'll do all I can to stop you marrying Despenser, at all events," said Ben.

"No, it's too late. Nothing can keep me from Neil now."

I heard Peter take a swift noisy breath. He began to speak. I motioned him to be quiet.

Lily started to laugh, quietly at first, and then her voice rising higher.

Ben leaned over and slapped her face hard.

It was the first explosion of the violence inside him. Lily gave a sharp short scream and then was silent, holding her cheek.

"That's on a par with your usual stupid reaction to a crisis," said a cold voice from the archway.

"Dad," said Peter, turning towards him. I stood where I was.

"Just now you were running away," said Neil to Ben. "Why didn't you keep on running?"

"I've had another idea," said Ben. "A better one. I don't believe there's anything to run from. Who's going to believe anything the neurotic, fantasy-ridden Miss Barclay tells them?" He glanced at me maliciously. "And Lily? We all know Lily's practically certifiable now."

Lily gave a little cry.

"Underneath everything, you're really just a lout," said Neil contemptuously.

"And Peter won't say anything," said Ben. "He won't talk. He hates you, did you know that? You are his parent and he hates you. He thinks you're an ironhearted father who destroyed his mother and doesn't trust him. And he isn't far wrong, is he?"

Neil just looked at his son without a word. Peter's face had a lost bewildered look.

"And don't blame me for it. I only stepped in where angels fear to tread. You did it yourself. You broke him. He's in pieces. And he's all yours. Every twisted bit of him."

"*No!*" Peter gave a wail and charged forward.

Ben threw him back with an angry push to the chest and the boy fell back against me, gasping and winded. Inevitably I stumbled backwards dragging Peter with me. As I picked myself up I saw Ben's cigarette lying on the ground. It was near the puddle of petrol I had noticed earlier. I opened my mouth to call. But before I could do so there was a glisten of light, then a sheet of fire and a roar. As I instinctively covered my eyes, I felt someone grabbing me and pulling. There was a smell of burning. Flames seemed to spring up in my body as if they were growing there. I was on fire. I opened my mouth and screamed.

Then blackness.

My next coherent memory is of lying on the grass outside St. John's and seeing smoke float above me. There was a strange smell in my nostrils. Somewhere in that picture was Neil's voice; and then a woman calling out. I remember for a moment thinking it was perhaps me, and then hearing Neil say: "Lily, be quiet." And then to someone else, he said: "Help her away."

When I was really myself again, I was in bed in a light room and it was sunny. I seemed to be in a hospital. A white-uniformed woman bustled in with a tray of breakfast and I struggled to sit up. I felt quite well, but odd, distinctly odd.

"I'll give you a pillow," she said. "And then you eat this."

"I'm very hungry," I said weakly, looking at the small tea-pot and single slice of toast.

She made a clucking noise, "I expect I can get you a boiled egg," she said, and started to depart.

"Wait a minute, can I have a mirror?" I said rapidly.

"Oh, you don't want a mirror," she said, banging the door behind her.

I passed my hands trembling, over my face. I couldn't

tell what was wrong with me, but I knew something was. Somehow, the last of my looks had gone.

She seemed a long time getting the egg. I don't know, perhaps I slept again. But I was still lying there and the tray had gone when I looked up to see Lynn Alloway standing my my bed. She was wearing a plain dark blue dress and her hair drawn straight back, but she looked more beautiful than ever. She put a cool finger on my arm.

"Don't disturb yourself. Just came in to say goodbye. You *have* had a rough time."

"Tim——" I began.

"Oh, Tim's fine now, just fine. But we thought a little holiday, say in Italy, would be a good idea. We have had a little coolness between us, Tim and I, but it's all over now." She smiled brilliantly and touched a sapphire and diamond ear-ring. "Happy families again."

"How *is* he?"

She patted my arm. "I must tell you, my dear, that Tim's made a little confession to me that he largely brought on his own illness. He's always been a tiny bit of a hypochondriac, has Tim. Especially," she added thoughtfully, "if he can't get his own way."

"But what about the arsenic?"

"Oh, I think that was just part of Dr. Ben's fiction, don't you? I've been hearing stories about all that. It *is* sad about Ben." For the first time her brilliance dimmed. "Really sad. I *liked* him."

"So did I."

"Anyway, no arsenic, as far as I know. If my Tim *did* have any arsenic, I bet he took it himself. Probably read somewhere that it improves your virility." She giggled softly.

"How do I look, Lynn?" I said bluntly and suddenly.

She blinked. "Oh well, you look a little rough *now*, chérie, but don't *worry*. After all, you can do so much about it these days, can't you?"

"Can you?" I said unhappily, my worst fears confirmed. I must be a monster. This was how people like Lynn cheered up the deformed.

Lynn got up to go. "I said once I'd tell you something about your appearance. That scar down your face; it looks

168

like the remains of an old wound, very very faint and far away, you can hardly see it. It makes you fascinating. Not perhaps to all men, but to many. They wouldn't admit it, but with it you attract them madly."

I stared at her. "Oh?"

"Yes." She paused at the door. "Don't let it be all jubilation. If you work on it, it's a lousy thought."

I lay back on my pillows, working on it, and it was indeed a lousy thought. I didn't want to excite anyone in the way Lynn Alloway spoke of. I felt I hated her informed sexuality. Also, she was too gay by half. I wasn't quite sure I believed her story that *no* arsenic had been fed to Tim Alloway. I wouldn't put it past Lynn Alloway to have had a go, yes, and to try again some time.

The door opened again and I hardly bothered to look up. But I knew who it was, of course.

"Hello, Neil," I said.

He came over and sat beside me.

"Sorry I was bad about Lily," I said. "I see now you were trying to look after her. Protect her."

"No one can protect Lily, really," he said. "A strange girl. In some ways so innocent and guileless, in others so acquisitive."

"Yes," I said, thinking of my aquamarine. "She takes what she wants all right, if that's what you mean."

"Your brooch? *Our* brooch, because it was my gift to you. I made her restore it. She's like a child. That's why it was impossible, of course, to let her have a child."

"A child?" I looked at him.

"Yes, that was the beginning of it all, I suppose. Or the beginning of the bad part. Until then it had been a simple boy and girl love affair."

"So it wasn't simply a matter of Lily believing herself to be Ben's wife," I said slowly. "If she really did believe it."

"Who can know what really goes on in Lily's mind? But what happened was that she became pregnant and Ben, who was a very young medical student, managed an abortion for her. Whether he did it or that nurse of his, I don't know. Together, I suppose. And it was the abortion that young Robert Madden got to know about."

"But why did I never hear *anything*. Not a rumour of it ever got to me."

"You were away, my dear, with those stone-faced German relatives of yours, and then in America, and by the time you came back it was over."

"But you didn't know either?"

"No. Not at first." He looked out of the window. "It was the year Antonia died. Later, when I took responsibility for Lily, I did wonder. But it wasn't until Lily herself recovered enough to talk to me that I heard the full story." His face looked grim. "I felt like whipping Ben, but I had to make sure first. Lily *could* have been in a state of delusion. So I hired a detective."

"Thank you for the roses and for Jackson," I said. "They were all you, weren't they? I can see Jackson might be your idea of a watchdog. He certainly has excellent hearing."

"The flowers were for love," he said.

I looked at him then. And unexpectedly, at least to myself, I smiled. "I suppose you thought I'd make a good stepmother for Peter."

"Oh rubbish." He took my hand. His touch, unlike Lynn Alloway's, was warm and firm. "How are you? How's the head?"

"No pain," I said warily. "What happened to me?"

"Shock, mild concussion. You hit your head when Ben dragged you out. It was him. I wish it had been me. But I had that wretched Lily hanging round my neck. And Peter, of course, was like a wild thing." He looked away. "In case you're wondering, Ben didn't get out. The old stables burned out and he went with them. I believe he went back in again quite deliberately."

"I think I guessed he was dead. He was a bad influence on Peter." But Peter had turned against him in the end.

"So I'm learning." He looked grim. "One way and another I haven't been so good either."

"You tried."

"The wrong way. Still, I chalk it up to my credit that I was suspicious of Ben. I began to pick up bits and pieces of talk that I didn't like. And of course, for a long while I had been trying to work out what really happened to young Madden. I didn't like the way suspicion of I don't know what seemed to be centring on Peter. Or if not Peter, then you. When I heard about the fire I was truly terrified for your safety." He paused. "You as a scapegoat and Lily silenced forever, that's how it could have been. Or else married to Ben. As far as Ben was concerned either went. Well, the detective stopped that. I'm sorry about his questions but he knew you'd talk to Ben."

"Yes," I said. "James Dilke. He frightened me." But it was not he that had frightened me, but my own imagination worked upon by Ben. Ben had come very close to breaking me. I saw that now.

"But why did Ben, of all people, want to treat me like that?" I said. "It seems so cruel. So pointlessly malicious."

"It wasn't without point," said Neil. "He hoped to drive you into his arms. I think he rationalised it to himself, even if he only thought of it as greed for your money. But basically what he did was completely irrational, and probably had its roots in a desire to dominate you."

"I often felt that he wanted to punish me," I said. "As I suppose, in a way, I was always punishing him when he saw my face." My hand went to my scar. "And yet, he *was* fond of me." I suppose it all hung together. After all, you only want to punish someone who has power over you.

"I blame myself for Lady Madden's death," said Neil. "I tried to protect her and Lily. I thought that if I could keep them apart then no crisis would arise. I planned to send Lily to Scotland with Mrs. Mac."

"Is she there now?"

"They have travelled up today. Mrs. Mac has her own house there. It's on the west coast just north of Glasgow. A great place for gardens," he smiled.

"So Lily will be happy," I sighed. "Poor Lady Madden."

"Do you know, I don't think she would have minded going suddenly like that. It wasn't such a bad way to die for someone who was always looking for oblivion. And she's had her revenge."

I looked at him. "I've always been afraid of fire," I said. "Tell me how Ben died."

He held my hand and I knew he meant to shield me from the obscene details of Ben's death. I stared intently

171

at his face trying to read through his words to the realit
of the charred bones, the blackened flesh, the incandescen
hair. I felt I owed this one last act of love to the Ben with
whom I had grown up.

The words "no pain," and "anaesthetic effect" an
"very quick" filtered through my consciousness. Then
felt Neil give me a gentle shake.

"Anny," he said. "Stop it. Don't let it obsess you."

I pulled my mind back from the flame and the smoke

"Because I love you, Anny."

"Yes," I said. "It's a reason."

We sat for a moment, hand in hand. "Is Peter all right?
I said, after a while.

"Yes. He's gone to London to do some work on earl
flying birds in the Natural History Museum."

"Pterodactyls?"

"Yes. He's confessed to me that Lady Madden gav
him the tip to clear out. He ought to have come to me
really, but as you know, he and I haven't been a very goo
team."

"I blame you for that," I said.

"Quite right. Well, I'm trying a new way. You know
he's quite a rich boy. His godfather left him a good capita
sum of which I am trustee. Peter's mature about money
So I said to him: Right, you don't like the idea of school
you're too young for college, and you don't want to sta
at St. John's, here's a thousand pounds of your own mone
and your freedom. What are you going to do with it
And he said he wanted to do a study on the evolution c
birds. So he's lodging in London and working there."

"What would you have done if he'd said he was goin
to finance a pop group?"

"Said no, I expect," said Neil with a grin.

Then I had another thought. "How did you and Jame
Dilke ever hear all Ben's invented stories? They had n
objective reality, and *I* never told you about them."

He smiled. "I had an ally."

I looked at him suspiciously, and was suddenly en
lightened. "Mrs. Twining! I always knew she listene
at doors."

172

"She's madly inquisitive. Also she found you an interesting study in psychology."

He didn't laugh as I had expected. Instead, he dropped my hands and straightened his back.

"Anny, I'm thirty-nine, I own St. John's with two hundred acres of farming land. I have an apartment in Paris of which I also own the freehold. As you know, it's just behind the Palais Royal and it's probably a valuable investment. I have an income from investments which makes me comfortably off. I can settle enough on you to make you secure. That's the business side of it."

"Thanks," I said breathlessly.

"I can give you social position in the county, for what that's worth. To you, nothing, probably."

"And what can I give you?" I asked.

"Your mind and your heart and your body."

"And will you give me the same? For as long as you can? I don't approve of short marriages."

"Forever," he said. "In spite of all the ladies who think I'm a middle-aged roué with a mistress in every city."

"They're far too sophisticated to use language like that," I said. "And they find you deeply interesting. I must say I shall enjoy being married to you."

"I'll get you a ring," he said. "I've already been into Garrards looking at one."

"No," I said. "I'll wear my aquamarine. You gave it to me and I love it."

Suddenly I didn't feel strange or unnatural any more. I touched my hair. "What is there about me? I thought I was terribly disfigured somehow, but I don't feel ill."

"Don't you know? Can't you tell?" He started to laugh gently. "You ought to see yourself."

"There's no mirror."

"I'll get one." He disappeared and soon returned bearing a small square looking-glass. "Sister let me have this."

I stared at my reflection. I saw my face, pale, huge-eyed, but clear and unmarked. However, around my head stood out a fringe of scorched frazzled locks. I looked like the victim of a bad hairdressing accident.

"My hair! It got burned."

"It doesn't look half bad," he said, appraisingly. "You look forlorn but delicious."

I remembered the seed of doubt Lynn Alloway had planted and I clutched his hand. "Neil, my face, my scar, you don't find me attractive *because* of it."

"What scar?" he said. "I never think of it. It really no longer exists except in your mind."

I smiled; it wasn't quite true, but perhaps it would soon become the truth. I had noticed that life works like that sometimes.

A puff of warm sweet air blew through the open window and ruffled my hair. I put up a hand to smooth it. During all the days when I had been full of fear I had also had moments when I wanted to laugh and dance, when my body couldn't help being happy. Heavy with despair I had carried within me a happy girl. Now I knew why. My future happiness, riding slightly ahead of me, westward like the sun, had reached out to warm me.

"Seen all you want?" He took the mirror away. "Just order yourself one or two wigs. Lynn Alloway has several. Ask her."

"I'll choose my own wig-maker," I said, and smiled again, thinking that, after all, he didn't know as much about women as all that.

FAWCETT CREST BESTSELLERS